FOR THE LOVE OF ANNA

Dixie Lynn Dwyer

MENAGE AMOUR

Siren Publishing, Inc.
www.SirenPublishing.com

A SIREN PUBLISHING BOOK
IMPRINT: Ménage Amour

FOR THE LOVE OF ANNA
Copyright © 2011 by Dixie Lynn Dwyer

ISBN-10: 1-61034-241-0
ISBN-13: 978-1-61034-241-4

First Printing: January 2011

Cover design by Jinger Heaston
All cover art and logo copyright © 2011 by Siren Publishing, Inc.

ALL RIGHTS RESERVED: This literary work may not be reproduced or transmitted in any form or by any means, including electronic or photographic reproduction, in whole or in part, without express written permission.

All characters and events in this book are fictitious. Any resemblance to actual persons living or dead is strictly coincidental.

Printed in the U.S.A.

PUBLISHER
Siren Publishing, Inc.
www.SirenPublishing.com

DEDICATION

I would like to dedicate this book to my husband and our wild and fun nights on the ranch.
"Love ya darling."

FOR THE LOVE OF ANNA

DIXIE LYNN DWYER
Copyright © 2011

Chapter 1

Anna exited the commuter bus. She'd had a long, hard day at the restaurant and couldn't wait to get home to soak her feet. She glanced at her watch as she walked down Main Street and 5th. It was one o'clock in the morning. He shouldn't be home yet, or if he were, he was probably out cold in a drunken stupor. Anna sighed in annoyance, then cringed. She needed to be more careful. If she made the mistake of talking back to her old man then he would surely lash out at her again. Hank Parker was a big, mean man, and when he was drunk, he was out of control.

Anna was petite, and one shove from a man her father's size would do serious damage.

She instantly thought about last week and how she refused to give him more money for liquor. She was tired. She had worked a month of double shifts getting four hours of sleep a night just so she could pay the rent and food bills. Her dad never paid the landlord. He just pocketed the money and went out drinking. She shook her head at the thought. It made her so damn angry because she was the one working her ass off to support them. Meanwhile, he didn't do shit!

She released an exasperated sigh as the anger dissipated. What good would it do her to get upset all over again? *Haven't I learned my lesson about talking back to my old man?* Flashbacks of that fight entered her mind. She would always remember every hit and every painful word her father inflicted upon her. She wiped a stray tear from her eye, demanding no more to follow. But the memory of the last fight fought its way to her mind. His face, his slurred speech, and the way he looked at her as if she was the most disgusting and terrible daughter alive, sent chills through her body.

When she accused him of taking the money for drinking, he backhanded her across the cheek and sent her flying into the wall. She was dazed for a few seconds, or at least it felt like that, and when she opened her eyes, her dad was consoling her.

Does he love me? She knew alcoholism was a disease, one that takes over a person, even those with the kindest hearts. When she thought about it, her father had never been kind. Drunk or sober, he hit her.

She gulped so hard it hurt her throat. She should listen to her best friend Stacy and just leave. Stacy offered a place to stay out in Texas, but Anna didn't want her pity, and she knew her dad needed her. He hadn't worked in over three years, and her paychecks paid the rent and the groceries.

She promised Momma.

Her vision blurred as the tears stung her eyes. Anna focused on getting home and sleeping as long as she possibly could.

* * * *

Their crappy apartment complex was just around the corner. Anna had paid the landlord yesterday, so she didn't have to use the back entrance to avoid seeing him.

Thoughts of a hot bath filled her head as she entered the front door. There was no security, hardly any working lights, and the place reeked of garbage.

As she ascended the stairs, her stomach began to quiver. She was frightened of her father, and the anticipation of his state if he was home was getting the best of her.

Quit worrying and move faster, she told herself as she reached the third floor.

Anna reached her door and placed the key in the lock. It had been left unlocked, and she cursed her dad under her breath. When would he learn to stop drinking and gambling and just be her father? She was tired of being the responsible one, and she was only twenty-three.

As she entered the apartment, she closed the door and threw her purse onto the couch.

"We've been waiting for you, little Parker."

Anna screamed and jumped backward at the deep voice. Two strange men in suits stood in front of her.

Instinct kicked in, and she bolted for the door.

Large, solid hands wrapped around her waist and easily lifted her off her feet and back in front of the other man. She didn't recognize either of them.

"Let me go!" she screamed, and the man holding her covered her mouth with his hand. He held her like a rag doll. It was useless to fight him, and she knew it. Both of them were mean and ugly, standing at over six feet tall.

She kicked and squirmed until he pressed his body against hers, holding her still.

"Quit fighting, little Parker."

She calmed down and waited to hear what they wanted.

"Good girl," he whispered next to her ear. The smell of liquor and cigarette smoke made her cringe in disgust. The other man moved closer.

He had a shadow of a beard and dark eyes, but it was the evil within them that showed perfectly, causing her to tremble in fear.

"We're not going to hurt you," he whispered before gliding his thumb across her bottom lip. She noticed the square, shiny ring covered in many small diamonds on his pinky finger. That had to have cost a fortune.

"Yet," whispered the man behind her, holding her closer, he was practically crushing her ribs.

"Where's your old man?"

"I…I don't know." She shook with fear at the way the man in front of her stared at her body. The man behind her squeezed her tighter.

"Please, you're hurting me," she whimpered as he chuckled behind her. His hot breath burned against her hair.

"I'm only going to ask you this once. Now be a good girl and tell us where your father is?"

"I don't know. I swear I don't know."

He stared at her as if contemplating whether he believed her or not.

She prayed he did. She prayed that they wouldn't touch her or hurt her.

"He owes us thirty thousand plus interest. He's way behind in his payments, and time is up."

Anna swallowed the lump in her throat. She instantly thought about the time two weeks ago when she found her father beaten, bloody, and drunk by the front door. She figured he drank too much and had a fight in a bar somewhere. Boy, had she been wrong. She was sick and tired of living this life and having nothing.

"I'm afraid if he doesn't show up, we're going to have to leave him a message. Unfortunately for you, it's going to be a very clear and precise message that he can understand." He rubbed the ring against her cheekbone. Not enough to cut her skin, but the threat was apparent.

"I swear I don't know what you are talking about. I work all day and night and give him the money for the rent and the food shopping. I didn't know he borrowed money. I swear," she yelled, and he grabbed her face so tight she felt pain in her jaw. She squealed as his fingers dug deeper into her cheeks.

"It's a shame that my partner here has to mess up this pretty little face, sweetheart." He shoved her face to the side, but his eyes remained on her.

"She's got quite the body, too," the guy holding her whispered, then grabbed a handful of her backside.

Anna screamed and tried to pull away, and he hurt her when he grabbed her rear. She clawed at the man behind her and kicked the man in front of her. Screaming, she attempted to run but was hit in the shoulder blade from behind.

"Bitch!" She heard one of them yell. Then she felt pain as the man who had been holding her backhanded her across the mouth. Strike after strike, she attempted to defend herself, rolling to the floor in a fetal position.

They kicked her ribs, and she felt the impact of each hit.

She cried in agony as their kicks lifted her off the floor, sending her farther across the room. Someone had to have heard her screams. *Oh, please, someone help me!*

"Hey, what's going on!" She heard her father's voice and erupted into a deep, painful cry. He would save her. He was her father.

The one guy grabbed her dad and closed the door before shoving her father up against it.

"Where's the money!" the man with the facial hair yelled.

"I...I ain't got money," her father stated as he pulled out the inside of his pockets in his pants, revealing lint.

The other guy started beating on him.

"You owe us money. A lot of money and our boss wants it now."

"I don't have anything. I need more time."

"We gave you more than enough time."

Anna cried out in pain as the other goon grabbed her off the floor. Her head throbbed, and her body ached everywhere. Her father wouldn't even look at her.

"Get the money by tomorrow, or we take your daughter for a down payment."

The men looked her over as if she were edible.

"She'd make a nice profit," the one guy stated.

"With her body, looks, and age, we'd have the old man's debt paid off within a few weeks," the other man added, then licked his lips before sniffing Anna's hair. She pulled her head away, and he jerked her body back up against his.

"No! Daddy, please. Help me, please. Give them something. Where's the thousand dollars I gave you this week?"

He wouldn't look at her.

"Daddy," she cried, and he looked at each of the men.

She was terrified at the thought of the men taking her.

She looked at her dad as she held her side, the pain increasing with every breath she took.

"Take her. I don't want her."

Anna felt her whole world crumble. Her father didn't love her at all. She wasted all this time, all these years caring for him, and for what? So he could whore her out to pay his gambling debts?

"Please don't do this." She pleaded with the men to leave her.

The one guy pulled her to him, caressed her arm, and then slowly caressed her throat, holding her closer against his chest.

"She's a real looker. Big tits, firm, round ass, and innocent. I can tell." He chuckled then he rubbed his hands across her breasts, squeezed, then glided his hand to the V between her legs.

She shook in fear.

"I may just have to break her in so she can be a real good cash machine for the boss."

Tears streamed down her face as he pressed his erection against her back. She wouldn't be able to fight them off. They were big men and used to using their strength and fists to get their way. Anna knew she was as good as dead if she didn't get out of there.

She needed to do something. She needed to escape. Her body shook so hard her teeth chattered. She needed to be strong. She was on her own, that was obvious. Anna lifted her eyes toward her dad, and her heart ached. He wasn't even in the room.

The thought of what her father did and how easily he gave her up caused bile to rise in her throat. It burned a streak straight to her stomach.

Think, Anna...think.

She felt his hot breath then his lips against her neck. When she tried to push away, he grabbed her throat and squeezed. His other hand pressed against the zipper of her jeans. He had the button undone and was working on the zipper. *Oh, God, please help me.*

"Please..." she barely got out.

He released his hold on her neck but kept her body against his. He kept rotating his hips and touching her everywhere. When he grabbed at her breast, ripping through the fabric of her blouse, he scratched her skin, and she cried.

"I have some money stashed in my room. If I give it to you, will you give us a few days to get the money my father owes you? I can ask the guys at work. They like me, they'll help me." She knew she babbled, but she needed to get to her room. She would escape out the window and get the hell out of town.

He paused a moment, and she pressed the palms of her hands against his chest. He was a combination of muscle and fat, the stereotypical wiseguy gangster.

The other man pressed against her, holding her hips while he rubbed his crotch against her ass. She was trapped between them, and panic set in. She nearly began to hyperventilate. Then she heard his question.

"How much you got stashed?"

She heard her father in the background.

"Anyone want a drink?' She cringed, and the tears burned her eyes. The bastard was getting a drink, and she was about to be raped by two criminal gangsters. Anger and determination felt like they burned through her blood.

"How much?" The other man repeated the question, squeezing her hip bone, grabbing her roughly on her thighs.

"A few thousand," she lied.

"A few thousand! You bitch. You been holding out on me."

She turned toward her father to give him a piece of her mind, but he was already there and struck her across her cheek. She went flying to the floor. The other two men laughed.

It was horrible, and she wanted the floor to eat her alive.

"Please. I will give you all I have. Let me go to my room." She held her hand against her cheek. She felt the blood, and the pain in her body was increasing with every minute that passed.

She slithered across the floor. Her body was in so much pain, but she feared for her life. She needed to escape.

The men didn't move to help her up, and they didn't stop her either.

The ache in her ribs made it difficult to walk. Her face and body throbbed with every step, but as she finally stood, holding the doorframe for support, she walked closer to the room. When she entered the room and slightly closed the door, she felt relieved at the distance between her and the three men.

No one followed her inside, and the second she was there, she grabbed the box under her bed and headed toward the window.

Carefully peeking over her shoulder to make sure they didn't follow, she heard their laughter then an argument.

Lifting the window open, she crept out, closing the window behind her.

* * * *

Anna wouldn't look down. She just focused on surviving and putting this life behind her.

With each step, the tears leaked harder and faster, and the pain increased.

Finally, she made it to the first floor and jumped the last twelve feet.

Her ankle twisted, and she bit her lip trying not to scream as her bruised and battered body hit concrete. Just her luck. How the hell could she run in so much pain?

Someway, somehow, she limped quickly to the corner. She could smell their cologne on her clothes. Bile rose in her throat, but she pushed on.

She waved down the first cab she saw and got in. "Go, go, go!" she yelled and constantly looked over her shoulder then behind the car as they traveled away from her apartment.

"Where to, miss?" he asked, never looking at her.

"The airport, please," she stated in a quivering voice before sinking into the smelly leather seat and closing her eyes.

Chapter 2

"Get over here, honey. I want a good morning kiss just like you gave Eric," Max stated as he chased Stacy around the bedroom.

She screamed in delight as her man caught her around the waist.

Before she could protest, his lips covered hers, and his arms wrapped around her body, pulling her against his solid chest.

He was breathtaking. Both brothers, Max and Eric, took her breath away. A relationship with two men was the furthest thing from her mind when she arrived in Pearl. It was an amazing town filled with so many different types of people and families. She loved it instantly.

Everyone was friendly and outgoing. They had town barbeques, carnivals, concerts, and celebrations all year round.

Max released her lips and held her close. His gun holster rubbed against her hip bone, making her feel horny and aroused. She pressed her cheek against his chest and squeezed him.

Stacy yawned against his chest, unable to control its release, and Max laughed.

"You were tossing and turning a bunch last night. Something on your mind, doll?" he asked, showing off his adorable dimples.

Stacy avoided eye contact, especially with him standing there in his deputy's uniform.

He was so intimidating with it on. He wouldn't understand the bad feeling she'd had the last few days. She couldn't stop thinking about Anna. Something was wrong.

"Stacy," he whispered, gently caressing her chin with his thumb.

"It's silly," she whispered back, but he wouldn't let her turn away.

"Come on, baby. I'm not falling for that 'nothing' stuff, and neither is Eric. If he didn't have to be up at dawn, he would be here right now, just as concerned as I am."

"I feel foolish is all."

"Talk to me."

He pulled her across the room, sat on the bed, and held her between his legs. Gently, he rubbed the palms of his hands over her backside.

Stacy placed her hands on his shoulders and locked gazes with him now that he was sitting down.

"You'll think it's silly."

He raised one eyebrow and looked at her in a way that said "spill the beans or I'm gonna get mad." A mad Cantrell was a bad thing, especially when it came to Max and Eric's cousins Charlie, Wyatt, and Ben. They were forces to reckon with.

"You know that Anna and I are very close? We've always had a strong bond with one another?" She hesitated.

"Stacy. Come out with it."

"I think something happened. I think she's in some kind of trouble."

He immediately squeezed her and scrunched his eyes up.

"What can I do to help? You want me to call some friends back in New York? Wyatt knows a bunch of people."

"I...I don't know. Maybe I'm being foolish. If something happened, I'm down as the first person to call besides her dad."

"Yeah, like that asshole would even care," he responded, and she smiled.

"Thanks."

"For what?"

"For listening these last two years and knowing how important Anna is to me. She needs to get away from her dad. She needs her own life. A better life."

He continued to hold her.

"Why don't you call her?"

"I tried but didn't get an answer."

"Well, what about calling the restaurant she works in? Maybe they can give you more information?"

Her eyes widened.

She hugged him tight, then kissed his cheeks, his forehead, then his lips.

"You're such a smarty-pants, Deputy Cantrell."

Giggling, he pulled her back onto the bed and began moving her nightgown from her body.

"I've got fifteen more minutes before I have to be at work. Why don't y'all show me some luvin'?"

Stacy straddled his hips and unzipped his uniform pants, smiling wide and loving her man.

* * * *

Anna exited the small bus, relieved to finally end her journey and get to the town of Pearl. It was completely secluded but was quite stunning. There were blocks of numerous boutiques and specialty stores as well as a large diner and a food shopping center. The school was at the end of town, and the sheriff's department was smack in the middle.

She walked slowly. Her injuries were far worse than two days ago. She stared at the sheriff's department for a moment wondering if her father was looking for her. The tears stung her eyes. Foolish her. After what he did, she knew better than to think of him ever again. He was dead to her now.

She thought about trying to remember where Stacy said she lived, but she couldn't. She hadn't called before she hopped on the plane. She knew Stacy was there in Pearl. She expressed her love for the place and the fact that she didn't want to leave. Looking around, she understood why. It was a lovely town, quaint and clean. The smell in the air was fresh, unlike the city.

She hid behind large sunglasses and a sweatshirt. It had gotten her through the airport even when people asked questions. People stared at her injuries, and she lied, saying she was in a car accident. That seemed to ease their minds. However, she used the washroom in the airport to wash away most of the blood, and she used a twenty to buy a sweatshirt to cover the bloody T-shirt she still wore. But here, she stood out. People looked at her, immediately noticing the outsider. She needed to contact Stacy.

Anna saw the payphone and headed straight for it. Stacy would be able to help her.

Chapter 3

"Eric!" Stacy yelled as she ran from the house with tears streaming down her cheeks.

Eric immediately stopped what he was doing and ran to meet her.

"Stacy, what's wrong? Are you hurt?" he asked, rubbing his hands gently over her body. His cousins, Ben, a rancher, and Charlie, a vet, ran over to her as well.

Stacy took a moment to catch her breath.

"Anna's here. She's in town, Eric, and she sounds hurt."

"What do you mean 'hurt'?" Charlie asked. Stacy allowed the tears to flow freely. These men were her family. She loved them and knew they were good men.

"She wouldn't tell me. She said she had a car accident. But she's waiting for me to come get her in town. Can you come with me?"

"Let's go," Eric stated, pulling Stacy along with him to his pickup truck.

* * * *

"There she is!" Stacy blurted out as Eric pulled the pickup truck alongside the curb near the hardware store. A petite woman sat on a bench with large sunglasses and a sweatshirt pulled snug against her body. She looked so fragile, as if she were trying to hide.

Stacy jumped out of the truck and ran to her. Eric watched as the two women embraced and Anna cringed and bent over. She was obviously in a lot of pain.

* * * *

"You're hurt! What happened?" Stacy asked as she held Anna at arm's length.

"Car accident," Anna stated in a scratchy voice.

"Oh, my God!" Stacy froze as if she were thinking Anna's statement through.

"Wait. You don't drive a car."

"Exactly. I was on the sidewalk. Can we talk about this later? I'm so glad to see you," Anna stated, then pulled Stacy into another hug.

Anna pulled away and took a few steps back when she saw the large cowboy walk toward them. He was tall and lean, and she watched as he stuck his hands in his back pockets.

"Are you going to introduce me to your friend, honey?"

Stacy looked at Anna warily before she introduced the cowboy.

"This is Eric. Remember I mentioned him and Max?"

"Of course. It's nice to meet you, Eric."

She reached out her hand to shake his hand, and her sweatshirt came undone. She watched as his eyes widened, and she pulled her hand away to pull the sweatshirt tighter. He probably saw the blood. Her ribs were killing her. She had yet to remove her sunglasses. When she did, Stacy would flip.

"I'm sorry to be intruding like this. It was a last-minute decision, and Stacy has been begging for me to come visit. I'm sorry about how I look, but I didn't get to change after the accident, and I hopped on the next available plane out here. I've been traveling by bus and nearly missed the one coming this way," Anna rambled on as Stacy and Eric listened.

"Not an intrusion at all, Anna. Stacy told us all about you. I feel like I know you already," he stated as he placed a hand on Stacy's shoulder.

"Well, let's head back to the ranch and get you settled. Do you have any luggage?"

"Oh…no…they lost my luggage. I'm not sure I'll get it back," she replied, then nibbled her bottom lip.

Eric appeared to read right through her lie, but Stacy accepted it.

"Well, then no need to worry. I have plenty of things you can wear, let's head home."

* * * *

Anna looked out the passenger window in awe. The ranch was magnificent. There were men riding horses, cattle grazing in the pasture, and two very large, beautiful homes separated by a traditional-looking red barn. There were stables and training circles. It was so impressive. As they approached the first house, the smaller house of the two, she noticed a group of cowboys standing by the fence. Her heart throbbed in her chest. They were giants. She thought the cattle and horses were extra large, but these men were tall and built like gladiators.

Her stomach quivered, and her hands shook. Great, now she was going to have a complex about large men. One look at Eric and she knew she better get used to it. It seemed Pearl grew their men real big. If she kept her distance, she would be fine for the little time she stayed here.

As the truck stopped, Anna's heart continued to pound, and her head throbbed.

Slowly, as not to jiggle her ribs more than necessary, she cautiously exited the truck. Her movement wasn't lost on Stacy or her man, Eric.

Stacy took her arm.

"You're safe here, Anna. I promise you."

Anna felt the tears sting her eyes, but she swallowed hard and let Stacy help her.

"Everything all right?" someone yelled from the group of men, and Stacy kept walking Anna into the house.

"Honey, you two will be all right while I head back to work?" Eric asked.

"We'll be fine. Thanks for the ride," Stacy said, and they headed inside.

* * * *

"So what's the deal? Who's the kid?" Charlie asked.

Eric smirked. "That's no kid. She's Stacy's friend, Anna."

"Well, I guess when you're six foot four other people look like kids," Eric teased then took a look back toward the house.

"Damn! She a tiny thang? She the one from New York?" Charlie asked.

Eric mumbled a "yeah."

"Hey, what's bothering you?" Charlie asked, and Eric smiled. Leave it to his cousin to know him so well.

"Not sure, really."

"Well, it's obvious you're concerned, so spit it out."

Eric laughed at Charlie. He didn't beat around the bush about anything.

"Anna has bruises and cuts on her face that she's trying to hide behind big goofy sunglasses. She's favoring her ribs as well."

"What?"

"She said she was in a car accident."

"You don't believe her, do you?"

"No. I don't, and I'm hoping she'll come clean with Stacy."

"Do you think she'll let me take a look at her? Maybe she hasn't even seen a doctor."

"I doubt it. She was nearly ready to bolt when I showed up with Stacy and approached them."

"You thinking she may be in some kind of trouble?"

"I'm not sure. I'll see what Stacy says later."

"That's a good idea. Keep me posted."

"Sure thing."

* * * *

Stacy stood in the spare gust bedroom staring at Anna. She knew something was up but didn't want to question her in front of Eric. It was obvious that Eric picked up on Anna's uneasiness and the few white lies she told. Knowing that Anna would never lie to her, she knew she had to have had good reason. Now, watching Anna sitting on the bed and still wearing those goofy seventies sunglasses, she knew she needed answers.

Stacy closed the bedroom door and crossed her arms in front of her chest.

"Fess up, girl, or I swear I will tear you a new one!"

Anna clutched the sweatshirt to her chest and slowly pulled off the sunglasses. Anna began to sob.

"Oh, my God, Anna, what the hell happened, and don't tell me any bullshit about a car accident." She rushed to kneel in front of her and pulled her into an embrace.

Anna moaned in pain and pulled away. The pain obviously took Anna's breath away.

"You're hurt badly, aren't you?"

Anna tried to explain in between sobs.

"I don't know. I've been running on adrenaline. I just had to get out of there. It was so terrible."

"Shhh, honey, slow down. First things first. Do I need to call the sheriff? My Max is a deputy?"

"No! No police, no sheriff, no law."

"Okay, we'll discuss that later on. Now, have you seen a doctor?"

Anna shook her head.

"Damn, woman! What the hell are you thinking? You haven't received any medical attention, and you flew here from New York? Didn't anyone ask about your injuries or your clothes?"

"Car accident."

"And they believed that bullshit?"

Stacy stood up and began to pace.

"Was it your father? Did your father do this to you?"

"Please, Stacy. I can't. I just don't want to think about the whole thing. I had no place to go. I had to run and get out of there before they…"

Stacy began to cry as she saw Anna cover her face and sob. It was such a tormented sound. Her heart ached for her best friend.

"Okay, honey, first let's see the damage and get you cleaned up. No offense, but you kind of need a shower or something."

Anna laughed as she wiped her eyes, then lifted her arms to smell her pits.

"You're right. I do." She sniffled.

They both laughed, but Anna was serious immediately.

"I'm sorry to do this to you. Eric is real handsome, and I can tell he loves you."

"Don't apologize for anything. I've been trying to get you to move out here for years. Listen to your older and wiser best friend and let me take care of you."

"You're only two years older than me. That's not that much."

"It's enough, so you listen to me and let me take care of you."

"I love you, Stacy."

"I love you, too."

Stacy hugged Anna.

"Now, show me the damage, and I'll determine whether you need to see a doctor."

Stacy stood back as Anna slowly rose from the bed.

When she unzipped the sweatshirt, Stacy saw the blood.

She tried to stay calm, but anger shot through her veins.

As Anna painstakingly removed the sweatshirt, she saw the bruises and hand marks on her skin. Then she removed the shirt, and Stacy covered her mouth and cringed.

"Anna! Oh, my God, Anna." Stacy shook her head and began to cry.

Neither said a word as Anna tried to speak.

"I'm alive, Stacy. That's all that really matters right now."

* * * *

Stacy headed downstairs and into the large kitchen. She told Anna that she needed to see a doctor, and of course, she refused. So Stacy threatened her, and Anna finally agreed to let Eric and Max's cousin, Charlie, take a look at her injuries. Despite the fact that he was a veterinarian, Charlie had served in the war as a medic. He handled all the first aid around the ranch.

Stacy let the coffee brew and stared out the window over the sink.

She watched the men riding horses and saw Charlie and Ben.

The tears welled up in her eyes. What the hell happened in New York? She'd never seen Anna so frightened or so unwilling to discuss it with her. And those injuries were so bad. How the hell did she travel like that?

"Hey, darling, didn't you hear me?" Eric asked as he entered the kitchen.

Stacy jumped at the sound of the raised voice. She was so deep in thought that she hadn't heard him.

As soon as they locked gazes, the tears rolled down her cheeks. Eric was immediately in front of her, pulling her into an embrace.

She sobbed against his chest, and he held her tight.

"Talk to me, baby. How's Anna really?"

Stacy pulled away a little and wiped her eyes.

"She's hurt bad. I don't know the gist of it, but her injuries are bad. She hasn't had any medical attention. She refused, but I did convince her to let Charlie look at her."

"That's my girl."

"I think her father had something to do with it."

"Motherfucker!"

"Exactly. But she won't tell. All she said was that she was alive."

The tears flowed again, and Eric pulled her close again.

"Where is she now?"

"She's taking a shower. I told her I would get Charlie, but I think it's gonna be awkward. She won't talk about what happened, so we'll have to let Charlie know ahead of time."

"No need, Stacy. I heard."

They both looked toward the doorway, where Charlie and his brother Ben now stood.

"Well, why don't we make some lunch. That way, when Anna comes down, she won't feel uncomfortable," Eric suggested.

"That's a good idea. Who knows when she ate last. She seemed real weak and exhausted. I don't think she's slept since she left New York, but it's just a feeling," Stacy added, and when she looked at the men, they all had scowls on their faces.

"Please don't scare her, fellas."

* * * *

Anna felt a lot better after the shower. The scent of the men was nearly eliminated from her nostrils. It had been tricky and a bit painful to raise her arms and wash her hair, but she was determined to get it done herself. Even the water hitting her body caused pain. Her stomach growled, and she recalled the last time she ate anything. She was on the plane in coach and had a handful of peanuts and a soda. It was the last flight out to Texas, and from there, she took a bus. It had been a long journey of thinking about her life and what could have happened. The tears stung her eyes. Her father sold her without a bat of the eye.

She put on the T-shirt and lounge pants that Stacy had given her. Of course, they were too big and too long. She opted for the pair of shorts instead. Stacy was five foot six, and Anna was five foot two.

The one thing they had in common was their abundant breast size, so at least the top had room and the bra fit well.

Glancing at herself in the mirror, she felt as terrible as she looked.

"Car accident, my ass," she whispered and laughed, remembering Stacy's words.

She didn't want to bring trouble to their doorstep. Would the men come looking to claim her for the money her father owed? The men seemed dead set on keeping her for themselves. A chill ran through her body.

She hoped that the scratch across her breast wouldn't scar. It was bad enough that the memories of his touch would surely remain forever.

She grabbed the sweatshirt Stacy left her and put it on. There was bruising on her arms, her neck, shoulders…everywhere. Stacy seemed to trust this Charlie guy, so she had no choice but to trust him, too. Just as long as she didn't have to go to a hospital or see the sheriff.

Taking a deep breath, she slowly headed downstairs.

* * * *

"There you are! I was getting worried about you," Stacy stated as she headed toward Anna, leading her into the kitchen. Anna halted at the sight of the very large men in the kitchen. They stared at her, and she turned away.

"I'm not really that hungry. Maybe I'll just lie down a while," Anna said and tried to step away. Stacy firmly held her arm.

"Nonsense! When was the last time you ate?"

Anna shrugged her shoulders.

"Sit down here, honey, and make a sandwich before Charlie and Ben eat it all," Eric teased then smiled.

"We wouldn't do that, Eric," Charlie stated as he took a bite of his sandwich and winked at Anna. She listened as they teased one another, and she tried to force herself to relax a little. The other two men were gorgeous. Shaking like a leaf, she took the seat farthest away from the men. Every so often, she saw them watching her.

* * * *

Anna was a tiny thing, and Charlie could tell by the looks of the bruising on her cheeks and neck that they were very recent and not from a car accident. A feeling of protectiveness came over him. A glance at his brother Ben and he could tell he felt the same sensation. Ben's knuckles were white as he held the mug of iced tea. Lots of questions went through Charlie's head, but he knew he had to be gentle with Anna. Stacy felt that whatever happened was traumatic, and seeing Anna, he agreed.

She remained quiet and picked at her food. The bruising and cuts looked new, and his gut said they were days old. He noticed her hands shook and her coloring was poor. Instinct told him she was weak, probably fatigued from not eating and not getting treatment for her injuries. The fact that she sat so far away from them and cringed each time they spoke concerned him. If she was going to let him check her injuries, he'd have to help her relax a little. He decided to try and get her more comfortable with him.

"I'm a veterinarian and medic around here. I take care of all the livestock and the humans as well," he stated with a smile.

He watched as Anna nibbled on her bottom lip but didn't reply.

"Charlie here has a gentle touch. He's real good at healing animals and people," Ben stated with a smile, but Anna glanced his way, then turned toward Stacy, who rose from her chair.

When they were finished with lunch, Stacy and Eric began cleaning up.

"Anna, will you let me take a look at your injuries? Stacy is real worried about you." Charlie tried to remain calm. The truth was that he was scared out of his mind to see what injuries had been inflicted upon this beautiful, delicate young woman.

Despite the bruises, she was gorgeous, and the fact that she had them caused a knot in his chest.

"Of course she is going to let you look her over. She promised me," Stacy stated and eyed Anna.

"I'm really all right. I don't want to be a bother, and I think if I take a few aspirin I should be fine."

Charlie touched Anna's hand. "I promise it will be all right."

He was drawn to her large brown eyes. His insides quivered, and his crotch grew tight at the attraction.

Anna seemed to feel it as well as she lowered her long, dark lashes and pulled her hand away. She placed them on her lap and remained still.

"Anna, you promised me that Charlie could have a look. He won't hurt you. I swear he'll be gentle, and if you don't want him to continue, he'll stop. I want to be sure you're okay, honey," Stacy pleaded as she kneeled by her chair.

Anna whispered something to Stacy that Charlie couldn't hear.

Stacy smiled. "He's big, I know. All the men around here are, honey, but that doesn't mean they'll hurt you," Stacy whispered, then stood up from the table. Her voice had cracked, and she quickly turned away.

Charlie was angry at the thought that Anna was scared of his size and scared that any of them would cause her harm. There was a man involved with this, a dead man if he ever met him.

"I'll grab my bag and be back in a minute," Charlie stated as he and Ben headed outside.

* * * *

Charlie took his bag off the bench on the front porch where he'd left it. He didn't want to bring it into the kitchen earlier and scare Anna.

"I want to know who hurt her, who put that fear in her eyes," Ben stated from behind Charlie.

"I know, Ben. So do I, but you see how scared she is. She was shaking the whole time we were in the kitchen with her. I've got a real bad feeling."

"You think she's on the run from trouble?"

"What do you think?"

Ben was silent a moment as he looked out toward the fields.

"I think I want to protect her and keep her safe. She's beautiful, Charlie. She could be the one we've been waiting for."

"I know. Let me examine her and see how bad it is. Then we'll work at getting her to trust us."

"I'll stay nearby in case you need anything."

Charlie smiled as he entered the house.

If Ben was feeling the attraction to Anna as he was, then he wouldn't want to be far from her. Charlie knew that one day they would get their wish and find their woman just like Max and Eric found Stacy. They wanted that, too. He, Ben, and Wyatt knew that one day they would find a woman to share. They each wanted the same thing. They wanted a wife and a family. They each had learned through casual sex that something was missing. They each individually demanded control and submission in the bedroom, but together, making love to one woman was their dream. They had shared one woman once, and it hadn't worked out. She had been in it for fun, but there were no real connections between the four of them. It would take a very special woman to be able to handle their sexual appetites as well as love them and accept them as a package deal.

They had grown up in Pearl just as their parents had. From a young age, their parents told them they each had a choice to make when it came to love. No one pushed them either way.

They had started off with separate lives that eventually led them together on the Triple C. Charlie had gone off to war, wanting to do his part in the fight against terrorism. That had put quite the damper on his relationship with Wyatt and Ben. Ben downright told him off the day Charlie shipped out. Charlie smirked at the thought. When he had finally returned from the war, injuries and all, his brothers were there for him as if he had never left.

Their bond was strong, and one night, after years of one-night stands and discussions over sharing a woman, they gave it a try.

The sex was incredible, but the connection with the woman was all wrong. It was frustrating and complicated because Ben liked the woman and he and Wyatt didn't share the same feelings. That's when they realized that if they were going to share, then they would all have to be attracted to the woman and feel a connection immediately. It wasn't solely about sex. It was about love, emotion, and a feeling of completion. He could only hope that Anna could possibly be the one.

Anna was definitely a possibility. The simple fact that he and Ben felt the need to protect and comfort her was a step toward achieving their dream. It would take Wyatt's acceptance of Anna and a shared attraction for her to be their mate.

* * * *

Charlie placed his medical bag on the bed as Anna stood straight and stiff in front of him. He tried to make her feel comfortable, but it seemed to him that she was still very scared.

He towered over her, and he remembered her fear in the kitchen and that his size added to her discomfort.

He smiled, and she nibbled on her bottom lip. He had noticed that Anna did that when she was nervous. She was adorable, but he did his best to act professionally and not think about the attraction he felt. It was becoming increasingly difficult the more he thought about what her body would look like without the clothes.

He swallowed hard, then cleared his throat.

"Why don't we start off slow? I'm going to take your blood pressure and then your temperature. I'll listen to your heartbeat, and then we'll take a look at your injuries. How does that sound?"

"Okay," she whispered, and her voice cracked. It was hoarse and rough.

"Come have a seat here." He patted the bed, and she slowly sat down. He noted her contorted expression. She was obviously in pain.

Her hands shook as he took her blood pressure.

"It's a bit high, but that's understandable when you're stressed and in pain."

"I'm all right, really," she whispered, her voice low. His stomach cramped at how appealing she was without her even knowing it.

"So you keep saying. Why not let me be the judge…for Stacy's peace of mind?"

She nodded her head.

Charlie placed his hand against her cheek and instantly felt the warmth penetrate his skin. Anna stared up at him with big, brown, sad eyes like that of an injured doe. His chest tightened at the thought that even his touch put fear in her. Her skin was soft and supple. He wanted to caress it and pull her to him into an embrace, but he knew he couldn't. Not now. He lifted his hand then pressed gently against her forehead. She felt warm to his touch. He smiled, trying to reassure her that she was safe with him, but Anna immediately looked down to the rug to avoid his gaze.

Reaching back to his bag, he retrieved a thermometer. He took her temperature. The minutes that passed brought an awkward silence between them. He focused on her beauty and the need he saw in her eyes earlier, and his groin tightened. He tried to think of something to say, but Anna had yet to respond to any of his questions with anything other than a nod of her head. He removed the thermometer and found she had a low-grade fever.

"You have a fever, honey. More than likely, it's from the injuries and pain you don't have," he stated then winked. He felt the chuckle catch in his throat as he looked at her.

She stared at him as if trying to read his mind. She looked untrusting, unsure, and it made him feel sick to his stomach. How could he convince her that she was safe here and with him?

He rose from the bed and held his hand out to her.

"Now let's take a look at the injuries."

He examined her cheeks, her chin, and then her eyes. He tried not to touch the injured skin, but he couldn't help but trace the finger marks and bruising with his own hands. He knew immediately what the true culprit was. The hands that did the damage were as big as his.

His insides tightened at the pain inflicted upon her, and he wanted to know who had done it. He tried breathing slowly and remained calm for Anna's sake.

"These are going to get a bit uglier I'm afraid. Did you ice them after the…accident?" he asked, and she shook her head.

He touched her neck and gently tilted her chin up. It didn't take a doctor to see that a large hand had made the marks. Someone held her by the throat. No wonder her voice sounded rough and she clenched her eyes when she swallowed too hard. He closed his eyes and tried to calm his anger.

"You don't have to do this. I know it looks bad. I'll live," she whispered, her voice sounding worse the more she spoke.

He smiled and was taken aback by her concern over how he might take looking at her wounds. The sweet thing, if she only knew the thoughts that were going through his head right now. They weren't pretty, and he wished the bastard who did this was standing here right now.

He gently caressed her chin, then softly rubbed his thumb across her lip. He was careful not to get too close to the cut there.

"You're beautiful, Anna, and I'm not cringing at you. I'm angry with whoever did this to you."

She turned her eyes away from him as best as she could. He released her chin.

Standing in front of her, he looked at the bruising on her arms. There were obvious finger and hand marks. Someone really roughed her up.

"Anna, you're going to have to take off your shirt."

She inhaled and took a step backward. Her face looked flushed, and he could see beads of sweat across her forehead.

She teetered in place a moment, and he reached for her.

"Anna, are you okay?" he asked. Then he saw her take a step to the side, and her eyes began to roll a little. Immediately, he pulled her to him as she passed out.

* * * *

Charlie picked her up and carried her to the bed. She was light and soft. She felt perfect in his arms. He wanted to protect her and care for her and, mostly, make her smile. He was shocked at his thoughts.

Touching her forehead, she remained warm. He hoped that her fever wouldn't get worse. Perhaps it was from the slight rattling in her chest he heard as he listened with the stethoscope. Or maybe it was from her injuries.

Slowly, he pushed her shirt up and cursed at the sight.

"Motherfucker!"

"What?" he heard Stacy say from the doorway. He hadn't even heard her open the door.

He carefully pulled Anna's shirt down.

"She passed out. She has a fever."

"Oh, my God! Will she be okay? She won't go to a hospital. If I call an ambulance, she'll freak when she wakes up. What do I do?" Stacy covered her mouth and began to cry.

"I think you should go back downstairs, Stacy. I'm confident that I can help her. If she gets any worse, we'll have to bring her to the hospital. Promises or not, I want to do what's best for her," Charlie stated.

"Come on, Stacy, Charlie can take care of her. He knows what he's doing," Eric added.

"No. She needs me. I can protect her now that she's here. I won't leave her again."

"Honey, listen to Charlie. He'll come get us if he thinks she needs to go to the hospital," Eric replied, trying to calm her. Charlie locked gazes with his cousin, and it was as if Eric understood that this was more serious than Anna let on.

"Please take care of her, Charlie."

"Come on, Stacy," Eric whispered, taking her hand and leading her toward the door.

Ben now stood there as well.

Stacy and Eric went back into the kitchen.

"Do you need anything?" Ben asked.

"Yeah, actually, I could use your help. This is going to be difficult with her sleeping."

Ben stood next to the bed just staring at Anna.

"She looks so small and fragile," he whispered.

"She's special, Ben, I won't let her leave here. We need to protect her."

Ben leaned down and caressed her skin. Charlie watched as his brother noticed the culprit of the bruising on her face and body.

"Those are hand and finger marks. Who the fuck would do this to such a little thing?" he said with a growl.

"Take a deep breath, it helps."

"If I ever find the bastard, he's fucking cow dung."

"I'll need your help with this. I think she may have a couple of broken ribs."

"What?"

"Shhh. You'll wake her."

"I'm gonna give her a shot of something to help her with the pain and to sleep. That way, we can wrap her ribs and monitor her breathing. I'm pretty sure she didn't puncture a lung. She would be in a lot worse shape."

"Jesus!"

"I know, Ben. I know. Tomorrow, I'll try to convince her to get X-rays. I can call Doc Jones and ask him to keep it on the low. He'll help us out."

"We're going to have to tell Wyatt."

"I don't even want to think about what Wyatt will do when he hears about her injuries."

Charlie filled the syringe and carefully injected the medicine into Anna's arm.

He got the supplies ready to wrap Anna's ribs.

"Okay, Ben, you're gonna have to hold her up while I wrap this around her nice and tight. I don't feel right removing her bra. Prepare yourself."

* * * *

Ben tried to control his breathing as his brother suggested, but as Charlie removed Anna's T-shirt, the extent of her injuries was too much. The bruising and discoloration was horrible. There was some swelling and rounded marks that made him instantly think of boot marks. They must have kicked her thirty times.

Ben wondered, what the hell happened? He wanted to ask her a thousand questions. He wanted to know where she came from. Why someone would want to hurt her? He had so many thoughts.

He began to tense and grind his teeth.

"Hold her tight, bro, but don't squeeze her to death," Charlie reprimanded as he began to check the damage. From Ben's position, he had a full view of her voluptuous breasts. The bra was pink and lacy, and she smelled sweet like brown sugar. Her right breast was scratched, and a bruise ran across it, disappearing under the material of the bra.

"Did you see her breast?" Ben asked.

"Is this really a good time to be talking about her body?" Charlie asked as he began to wrap her waist from below the breast line under the wire of her bra. The bruising appeared worse by her stomach and lower ribs.

"No. I mean the one breast where there's a red scratch. It's deep and leads toward her…just check it out."

"In a minute, I'm almost done wrapping this."

Charlie finished up then helped Ben lay Anna back down.

She moaned in her sleep, and both Ben and Charlie locked gazes.

"The painkillers should begin to work soon."

Charlie stared at her a moment and saw what his brother had seen. He carefully inspected the scratch by her breast. Moving the bra away, he saw the bruising that led toward the areola. He covered her then pulled the covers up to her chest. His hands remained on either side of her, clenching the covers.

He was silent a moment as the thoughts filled his head.

"Do you think…do you think she was raped?" Ben asked, then closed his eyes and breathed.

Charlie saw his brother clench his fists as he kneeled by the bed.

"I don't know, Ben. I sure hope not. I'll have to ask her tomorrow."

"I want to stay with her. The guys can handle the last few hours."

"I'll go downstairs and tell Stacy and Eric what we saw and what our plan is. Call me if she stirs."

Ben nodded then pulled the large recliner closer to the bed.

Chapter 4

Charlie, Wyatt, Ben, Eric, and Max sat in the study. It was midnight, and they finally got Stacy to settle down in the same room as Anna.

"I think I should call a few friends in New York and see what we can find out," Wyatt stated as he sipped a snifter of brandy.

"No. Stacy said that Anna won't speak to the police or to you, Wyatt, as the sheriff. She's scared. Whoever did this roughed her up good. I've seen the damage up close. We need to make her feel safe," Charlie stated as he rubbed the back of his neck.

Wyatt exhaled. "Maybe if I have a talk with her tomorrow she'll feel comfortable enough to trust me. I am the sheriff, and I'll need to determine if there's a chance someone is after her."

"Trust is not going to come easy with that woman. The fear in her eyes as I examined her was gut-wrenching. I don't know how she survived the pain so long without meds."

"Yeah. Just about every spot on her body was bruised. I don't know how she made it here in one piece," Ben added, shaking his head.

"You're gonna bring her to see Doc Jones tomorrow, Charlie?" Wyatt asked.

He nodded as he rubbed his eyes.

"I want to find out who did this and kill the bastard," Ben stated very seriously.

"Join the club," Charlie responded.

"There'll be none of that. Let's just figure out what happened and help her to heal," Wyatt stated, sounding authoritative.

"Stacy said that Anna's father was abusive. He has a drinking problem, and Anna's been supporting them on her own for the last three years," Eric added.

Remarks flew through the room at the information.

"You think her old man did this?" Ben asked in shock.

"Not sure. Stacy was adamant about getting Anna here a year ago. She had been trying to convince her. They're real close, and last night, she couldn't sleep," Eric stated.

"Yeah, she was tossing and turning all night. She told Eric and me that she was worried about Anna. She knew something was seriously wrong," Max added.

"They must be real close for Stacy to feel that from a distance," Wyatt replied.

"Well, Anna did travel all the way here before even seeking medical attention. Thank God she got here safely."

Everyone mumbled in agreement before the room fell silent.

"There's something you guys should know." All eyes were on Charlie, and they heard the seriousness in his tone.

"Ben and I found bruising and a cut over Anna's breast. There were bruises everywhere. I didn't want to go lower. I'll let Doc Jones ask the questions."

"Son of a bitch! You think she was raped?" Wyatt asked as he stood up from his chair and paced the room.

"I don't know. She may have been, or she could have been manhandled so much that the bruises were everywhere. I pray she wasn't. The bruising is intense, and considering the size of the hand and fingers marks, I'd say the culprit was a large man. We won't know for sure until Anna confirms this."

"What kind of monster would lay a hand on a woman her size? On any woman for that matter?" Ben asked, and everyone shook their heads and mumbled comments.

"Let's see what Doc Jones can find out tomorrow. You all need to make her feel safe and keep an eye on her. I don't want to go snooping around until we know facts. The only way we are gonna get those facts is by questioning Anna. If she didn't trust you, Charlie, then I'm sure it's going to take some time. Let's see what tomorrow brings," Wyatt added, and the room went silent.

* * * *

The screams awoke him from his slumber. Charlie had insisted on staying the night in case Anna needed medical attention. He took the stairs to the second floor two at a time. When he got to the open door, he saw Eric and Max first. They looked white as ghosts. Max was running his hands through his hair, his eyes were glossy, and Eric didn't look much better.

The closer his steps took him into the room, the clearer the image came into view.

The light by the bedside table illuminated the room but not the corner by the bed and behind the recliner. Stacy was on her knees talking, whispering, and caressing something or someone behind the chair.

"It hurts…please, stop them…Daddy!" the voice screamed. It sounded so fragile and helpless.

Charlie slowly came around the bed and leaned down next to Stacy. She knew he was there but never took her eyes or her hands off of her best friend Anna.

Charlie watched as Stacy caressed Anna's leg.

"They're gonna kill me. I have to escape!" Anna shook with fear. Whatever had happened to her she was obviously re-experiencing it in her dream. The pain, the upset…everything. Charlie had to do something. His heart ached at the sound.

He got down on his knees in the small space on the floor and gently took Anna's hand into his own.

"It's Charlie, Anna. Stacy's friend, the doctor, honey…wake up, please. Come on, baby, you're safe here." His tone was gentle and caring as he caressed her skin. The sight of her curled up in a ball, clammy and crying, tore at his heart and soul. He worried about her injuries and the position her body was in.

"Stacy, let me pick her up and see if we can get her to wake," he whispered. Stacy looked at him. He saw the pain she was in and how upset she was getting seeing her friend like this.

Charlie saw Max help Stacy up and pull her into his arms.

Charlie slowly wrapped his arms around Anna, whispering and caressing her as he gently pulled her into his arms.

Her breathing was rapid, her chest blotchy and red as she cried her heart out.

"I've got you, baby, you're safe here with me. No one is going to hurt you ever again, doll," he whispered, holding her against his chest.

She was light and fragile in his arms, like a wounded animal, he took care of her and swore he would protect her as long as she was with him. She seemed to be calming down as she held his shirt in a death grip and snuggled closer.

She continued to moan and cry more softly when, suddenly, her eyes began to flutter open. "He doesn't love me. He never loved me."

The words tore through the room. Charlie caught the response from her words as he scanned everyone's eyes. Then he held Anna's gaze. He saw the fear, felt her cringe and try to pull away, but he wouldn't have it.

"Shhh now, baby doll. I'm here, and I'm not going to leave you."

"Anna, I love you, honey. Please let Charlie take care of you." Stacy caressed Anna's arms as she cried.

"Don't cry, Stacy. I'm sorry…I…I didn't mean for this to happen," Anna whispered, her voice barely audible to everyone's ears.

Charlie pulled her closer against his chest.

* * * *

Anna was relieved that she wasn't still a captive of the bad men back in New York. The nightmare was so real, she was embarrassed to find she obviously woke the whole house. It felt good to be in Charlie's arms. She felt safe, yet she was scared. The fact that she only had a bra on and a skimpy pair of shorts had her trying to wiggle free and cover herself. He had taken care of her earlier. She felt the bandage against her ribs and knew Charlie must have felt that she needed them wrapped. She was very tired as her eyes felt heavy, and she began to give in to Stacy's request that Charlie help her.

Charlie held her tighter, then sat on the bed, cradling her in his arms. Stacy placed a blanket over her body at Charlie's request.

"I'm sorry," she whispered one last time before closing her eyes. Her head hurt, and her body throbbed. The dizziness overtook her. She felt hot. Really hot. She couldn't help but think Charlie holding her was the culprit. No man ever held her. She never got this close to one and forgot about her father.

The thought caused a deep sob to escape her lips. Charlie pulled her closer against his chest and lay on the bed with her. "You're safe, Anna. Close your eyes, darling, and get some sleep."

* * * *

Anna awoke feeling warm, content, and very safe. Her face was wedged up against something big and solid that smelled like men's aftershave. The fear filled her immediately as she opened her eyes. *Charlie.*

He had stayed with her last night just like he promised. The feel of his hand pressed against her backside and the fact that her leg was wedged in between his should have made her try to escape and get away. She was afraid and had never been this close to a man before, let alone a man as big as Charlie.

She took in the sight of him, and her heart pounded against her chest. He was handsome in a John Cusack kind of way. His hair was sandy brown and a little long, but it did him justice. She remembered his eyes were light brown, like extra light brown sugar, not the dark kind. And his body, his body was muscular and large. She felt like a small child in his arms, yet her body was filled with lust like a wanton woman.

She released an exasperated breath, and he stirred. She stilled in his arms and closed her eyes.

"Oh, God," she heard him state as he slowly removed his hand from her backside and gently pulled her leg from between his.

She played possum for a few seconds while he gathered himself, cursing under his breath and pulling his arms away from her so that he wouldn't be touching her body so intimately.

She had to submerge the giggle and giddiness she felt. That was immediately replaced by loss. Slowly, she opened her eyes. His smile lit up her heart.

"Good morning," he whispered. She scooted away from him.

He touched her hip, gently stopping her from moving farther across the bed.

"No, please stay where you are. I promise nothing happened. I didn't try anything," he stated.

"You didn't?" she asked, raising her eyebrows in challenge.

"No. I held you in my arms all night. I wouldn't do that to you."

He touched her forehead, and she closed her eyes. The feel of his skin against her skin warmed her heart. He was caring and compassionate the way a man should be to a woman.

She felt her body tense, and he immediately rose from the bed.

"Your fever broke."

She stared at him and pulled the covers to her chest as the cool morning air replaced his warm body.

"I swear I didn't touch you, Anna. I wouldn't do that."

"I know," she whispered, but something told her that he didn't feel the same attraction that she did. She was inexperienced and insecure. He looked at her like he wanted to get as far away from her as possible. He was a doctor, and staying there with her was just him having a good bedside manner.

"I'm gonna head out. I need a shower and to check on the animals. My brother Wyatt is going to call Doc Jones. I want those ribs of yours x-rayed to make sure they're not broken and him to check you over."

"Who's Wyatt?" she asked.

"The sheriff, and my brother."

She nearly missed the "my brother" part because of the sheriff title.

She pulled the sheets tighter against her chest, shaking her head.

"No sheriff. No police."

Charlie walked back over to the bed and stared down at her.

"We need to get you checked out so I can help you. My brother will protect you just like the rest of us."

"I won't talk about what happened. You can't make me."

He sighed, then placed his hands in his pockets as if the conversation was too uncomfortable for him.

She closed her eyes.

"He'll be here by ten. I'll have Stacy help you, and she can go with you, too."

Anna wouldn't look at him, and as she closed her eyes tighter, she heard him exit the room.

Chapter 5

Taking a shower had been hell. Stacy had filled her in on the night she'd had, and Anna was utterly embarrassed. Thank god no one was in the kitchen by the time she and Stacy came down for breakfast. She made Stacy call Wyatt and tell him that she would bring Anna to the doctor. It took some convincing but worked.

They made their way out to the truck, and Anna quickly put the large sunglasses on to cover her bruises. Stepping up and into the truck took a great deal of effort due to the pain in her ribs. She prayed they weren't broken. She just wanted to heal and forget.

The ride was quiet and peaceful. Stacy didn't push more just drove into town.

When they arrived at the doctor's office, it wasn't crowded, so Dr. Jones saw her right away.

"Do you want me to come in with you?" Stacy asked.

Anna shook her head. She was a grown woman. She handled every obstacle and sucky thing that had occurred in her life because she was strong not weak. She wasn't going to be weak now.

She put on the yellow examination gown, surprised at the bright, nontraditional color. When she finally met Dr. Jones, he was cheerful and friendly just like the color of the gown and the decorations in the room. She was in a room with tropical colors and images of a beach scene. It was relaxing.

"Hello, Anna, I'm Dr. Jones."

Anna shook his hand as he took in the sight of her bruises. He smiled kindly, and Anna got the sense that he was a nice man. He talked to her about the town and the upcoming events in the months to come. It calmed her for the moment.

"I'm going to ask you some questions, Anna, and I want you to be completely honest with me so I can treat you. If you don't tell me everything, then I can't help you."

She locked gazes with him. She got a funny feeling in her stomach. Did he expect her to tell him what had happened?

She nodded in agreement.

"So, it's obvious someone roughed you up. There are bruises with the shape of hands and finger marks across your body, your face, and jaw, as well as your legs."

Anna swallowed hard as the tears filled her eyes.

"Honey, you're safe here. No one is going to hurt you. The Cantrells are very well known and very good men. They will surely keep you safe. Charlie has already done a great job." He smiled, and she felt a little more at ease.

He asked a few more questions, and with each response, she told him bits and pieces of the incident.

"Was it one man?" he asked.

"Three," she replied, and she saw a flash of anger in his eyes, but it was quickly replaced by tenderness.

"Honey, I know this is tough. You don't have to talk about it in detail, but I need to know so I can determine the extent of this exam. Did these men force themselves on you?"

She covered her mouth with her hand and shook her head in denial. All she saw were flashes of the men hitting her and then her father selling her like trash and hitting her himself.

Dr. Jones stood beside her and caressed her shoulder.

"Are you sure, Anna?" he asked again.

She wiped her eyes and locked gazes with him.

"I escaped…through the window and fire escape before…before they could." The thought that they would have raped her and forced her to prostitute had her sobbing again.

Dr. Jones consoled her, and before long, she was telling him what had happened. Including what her father said and did.

"The lousy bastard," he whispered, and she chuckled between sobs.

"Thanks for that."

He pulled her into his arms and hugged her. It was fatherly and comforting.

As he pulled away, he held her shoulders and locked gazes with her.

"You are a very strong and very brave young woman. You are sweet and kind, I can tell these things, I've been around forever. I didn't get these gray hairs from doing nothing." He winked.

"If you ever need to talk or need anything, you don't hesitate to call me. In the meantime, know that the Cantrells will protect you and care for you."

"Thank you," she whispered.

"Now, about Sheriff Cantrell."

Anna shook her head.

"Anna, these men were going to kill you and your father for money. They were going to take you and turn you into a prostitute to pay off the debt. They could come looking for you here."

Anna felt the tears stream down her cheeks.

"Then I'll leave here as soon as I can travel."

He shook his head.

"That's not an option, and you know it. You have Stacy and the Cantrells. You would be safest here. But with help from the sheriff, he can make some inquiries and ensure that these men don't come to Pearl to get you."

Anna thought about Stacy. She didn't want to bring trouble to her doorstep. They all had been nothing but nice and caring.

Anna lifted her chin toward the doctor. "I'll think about it." He released a sigh, then smiled.

"Deal." He smiled.

"Now, let's get the X-rays done and see where we stand there."

"Do you think they're broken?"

"We'll have to see. With the size of the men you described, plus your petite size, it's very possible."

"You ready?" he asked, holding out his hand.

She nodded, and he helped her down from the table.

* * * *

Stacy remained straight-faced during the ride back to the ranch. Anna wrung her hands together on her lap and stared out the window.

"Stacy?"

"Yeah?"

"I...I want to thank you for everything you've done for me. I had no place to go, and when everything happened, I got on a plane and just headed here."

Stacy reached over and patted Anna's hands.

"I'm glad you did, honey. I'm so happy you're here and that you're safe."

"Um...I know you're worried, and I just want you to know that I'll be okay. I survived, and I'll get through this."

Stacy was silent a moment and had been patient, not pushing questions on her, and she loved her for that.

"I know you want to know what happened and all, but I need time. Especially since I told Doc Jones everything, I feel kind of spent right now and really tired. I just think you need to know that...that they didn't rape me," Anna stated with her lips quivering, and Stacy caressed Anna's hands as she kept her eyes on the road.

"They?" Stacy asked, sounding angry.

Anna nodded.

Stacy clenched the steering wheel.

"Give me some time, and I promise to explain."

"You got it, honey. Let's head home so you can rest. I can't believe you have broken ribs."

"Me, either."

Anna smiled at the thought of having a home. But this wasn't her home, it was Stacy's and the handsome Cantrell men's home. She never really had a home, and the thought of ever having one seemed impossible at the moment.

She wiped the tears with the back of her hand and stared out the window at the stunning countryside.

She would love to live here. The town was quaint and lovely. The people were friendly, and the land was open and clean. There weren't horns honking, garbage on every corner. It was like something from a movie. Especially Dr. Jones, who was so kind and easy to talk to. People wished for doctors like him and towns like Pearl.

Granted, there were nice parts of New York City, but she lived in the shittiest. It was all she could afford. There was always trash by the entranceway, trash on every floor, and an elevator that never worked properly. She was shocked that the fire escape hadn't broken on her way down it.

Anna felt nervous at the memory. It was the scariest thing she had ever been through. She figured after that she would be afraid of heights for the rest of her life.

The closer they got to the ranch, the calmer she seemed to get. Talking to Dr. Jones seemed to make her feel a bit better.

Chapter 6

Stacy let the men know that Anna was all right. She eased their minds when she informed them that Anna hadn't been sexually assaulted. They had questions, especially Charlie, Ben, and Wyatt. Stacy couldn't help but think that the three Cantrells were attracted to Anna. They expressed concern for her every day, and any time they had free, they came by to check on her.

Anna seemed surprised that she had two broken ribs and five badly bruised ones. No wonder she was sick with fever and in such bad pain. They were amazed at her strength for baring it so long and flying in a plane, traveling to get to Texas with such injuries.

As the weeks passed, the injuries on Anna's face began to heal. With a little cover-up, they were barely noticeable anymore.

The sound of someone entering the kitchen pulled Stacy from her thoughts.

"Good morning," Anna stated as she walked over to the coffee pot and poured herself a cup.

"Good morning. How do the ribs feel today?" Stacy asked with a smile as she took a sip of coffee from her mug.

"Sore, but I guess considering it's not quite three weeks, it's going to take a while."

Stacy watched as Anna slowly sat down in a chair at the kitchen table.

Anna appeared deep in thought then spoke. "How about that walk today, so you can show me the river?" Anna asked.

Stacy swallowed hard. She had a feeling Anna was ready to tell her what happened back in New York. She had been very patient despite the men's push for her to get more information. She wouldn't do that to Anna. It was her story, her life, and she wanted Anna to always trust her.

"If you think you're up to it, I can pack a lunch, and we can picnic there."

"That sounds lovely, but I'm not sure if I can sit on a blanket and then get back up again. The thought of the pain makes me cringe." Anna chuckled as she scrunched her upper lip and nose.

Stacy smiled. "No worries, we have a table set up down there. We often picnic down by the water during the summertime. You'll see, in a few more weeks, the temperature will really change and be so hot. The spring is still a bit on the cool side."

"It's so nice and quiet here. You're lucky to have this place as a home."

Stacy joined Anna by the table, sat down, and took her hand into her own.

"This is your home, too, now."

Anna dropped her gaze to the table.

"I don't want to impose and outstay my visit. As soon as I'm healed, I think I'll move on."

Anna lifted her eyes, and Stacy was certain she could see the sadness in her eyes. Stacy quickly gained control of her emotions. Stacy patted her hand. "There's plenty of time to discuss this, no need to make any rash decisions now."

She rose from the chair and placed her coffee mug in the sink. She washed it and placed it on the drying rack.

* * * *

Anna felt sad. She didn't want to insult Stacy or push her away, but that was exactly what she was doing.

"I'm sorry," Anna whispered as Stacy remained facing away from her and toward the window.

"You don't have to apologize."

"I do, Stacy." Anna released a long sigh, and the tears filled her eyes.

"I feel so…numb," Anna admitted.

Stacy immediately turned toward her.

"I hurt…so much inside." Anna covered her face and began to cry. She hated every ounce of herself. She hated feeling defeated and worthless. Her own father didn't even want her.

Stacy pulled Anna into her arms.

"It will get easier, Anna. I promise, the longer you stay here and begin your new life, the better things will get. I love you."

Stacy and Anna looked up as she heard the floor creak. Charlie stood in the doorway, his eyes crinkled and a look of concern on his face.

"Is everything all right?" he asked, and immediately, Anna pulled away from Stacy as she wiped her eyes.

"Just some girl talk," Stacy replied, rising from the seat and heading back to the sink.

"You need a drink, Charlie?"

"No, Stacy, that's all right. I came by to check on my girl Anna." He smiled wide, and Anna felt that funny feeling in her gut again. He was a good-looking man, a cowboy, and would have his share of women pining over him. The thought made her jealous. What a moron. She was clinging to an imaginary attraction because he had helped to bandage her up while she was wounded. She needed to put a stop to it now.

"I'm fine, Charlie, and I appreciate you helping me out with my injuries. But, I don't…need looking after. You have important work to do on the ranch and…I'm not your girl. I'm not a girl…I'm…"

She paused, her words and what she wanted to say was all twisted inside.

The phone rang, and Stacy answered it, then left the room talking.

Immediately, Charlie took the seat next to her and scooted closer.

He placed the Stetson he held in his hand down on the table then looked her in the eye.

Slowly, he reached toward her face, brushing a loose strand of hair away from her eye.

His thumb caressed her lower lip as he smiled at her.

"I like calling you my girl."

She turned away and lowered her face, looking down into her lap.

"Look at me, Anna," he whispered, helping her by cupping her chin and tilting it up toward his face.

Charlie had long, hard fingertips but a gentle touch. She looked into his eyes, and her heart pounded in her chest from being so close to him.

"I like looking after you, and yes, I have responsibilities, but I can also check in on you whenever I want. I know that Wyatt and Ben will as well. We're gonna take care of you, so you best get used to it quick."

She shook her head. "I'm not staying here. As soon as I'm able to travel, I'm going to leave."

"No, you're not. You're staying right here on this ranch in Pearl."

"You don't understand. I don't want to intrude, and I don't belong here. I don't know if they'll come…" She quickly closed her mouth and tried to pull away. Charlie wouldn't let her.

"You don't know if who will come?" The sound of Wyatt's deep voice filled the room.

Anna immediately saw the uniform, and the tears filled her eyes. She pulled away from Charlie and stood up. Charlie stood up as well and immediately pulled her into his arms.

Anna swallowed hard.

The last thing she needed to do was inform a sheriff about the men from New York. That would be like attaching a homing device to her forehead along with a bull's-eye. No. She had to keep their identities a secret.

"Well?" Wyatt asked again as he eyed her from head to toe.

He wasn't as handsome as Charlie and Ben. He had a meaner looking expression. His facial structure was strong and defined. He had character but looked untamed. Even his nose wasn't perfect and showed it had been broken at least once. Yet, she was attracted to him as well. Any woman would look at him with the desire to tame him if she could. She wasn't that kind of woman. She had always been weak and powerless when it came to men just like these cowboys. It was how her father defeated her, broke her down with his name-calling and physical abuse. Wyatt was firm and persistent, and it intimidated Anna big time.

"I asked you a question, Anna."

She jumped at his tone, which didn't go unnoticed.

"Wyatt, you're scaring her." Charlie tried to intervene as he held her closer against his chest.

Wyatt moved closer to them. She swallowed hard at the sight of his massive chest beneath the fancy sheriff's uniform. His gun and holster sat on his hip just daring someone to make him draw. She had a feeling he was quick and good with a gun. The thought made her belly warm. His badge, his whole alpha male demeanor was filled with testosterone. He was a badass, and he knew it.

She was forced to look straight up at his six foot four body until she reached his eyes.

God, he was handsome in his own unique way.

He reached out to her, and she flinched before hiding her face against Charlie's chest.

She heard him swear under his breath, then place a gentle hand on her shoulder.

"I would never strike a woman, and I sure as hell would never strike you." His voice was firm and deep. He was so close to her she felt the warmth against her hair.

As Anna peeked up at him, turning her head across her shoulder, her lips hit his hand, and her insides quivered. It was like an electric shock against her skin.

He brushed a thumb across her cheek and stepped closer to her. Holding her gaze, he asked her again.

"You're afraid who is going to come here looking for you?"

She found herself answering his question.

"The men...the men who hurt me."

His thumb paused a moment at her lips, and she wished they hadn't. It felt so good to feel his touch. She noticed his jaw tighten, and nervously, she licked her lips. Both men seemed to shift.

"Why would they come here? What more do they want?" he asked as he held her chin in place.

She hesitated a moment and took an uneasy breath. The dark look in his eyes told her he always got the bad guy to confess. She was no match for his interrogation.

"Me," she whispered, and her voice cracked.

A tear rolled down her cheek.

"Aww, honey," Wyatt whispered. He brushed the tear away with his thumb then held her cheek in his hand. She leaned toward his warm touch, closing her eyes, letting the tears flow.

"We won't let them hurt you, Anna. I swear, my brothers, cousins, and I won't ever let them near you again."

Charlie pulled Anna into an embrace, and Wyatt placed a kiss on the top of her head.

She felt safe in their arms, and she felt an attraction to both of them. She was definitely one screwed up individual.

* * * *

Anna looked out across the small river to the fields of wildflowers in full bloom. It was peaceful there and private. Anna and Stacy sat side by side in chairs along the river's edge, neither of them speaking a word. They just enjoyed one another's company and nature.

Time seemed to slow down, and Anna felt at peace for the time being. It gave her strength and a bit of hope. She watched the birds land, find some worms, then take off again. She tried to see exactly where their nests were, and she wondered if there were babies there.

Taking a deep breath of fresh air, she allowed herself to feel safe and free.

"It's so quiet, Stacy. I never thought it would be possible to hear grass grow."

Stacy chuckled.

"You get used to it, Anna. Life here is so different from the hustle and bustle of the city. There's no need to rush, no need to ignore the simple things in life. I love it here. It calms me and makes me feel like I have my own piece of heaven."

Anna smiled. "A piece of heaven… I like the sound of that."

"Well, take your pick, honey. There are acres and acres of Cantrell land around these parts."

Anna smiled, thinking if it could only be that easy.

As she looked around her, absorbing the scenery, she thought about her life, the pain and the time she wasted. All she knew was that, at this moment, she could breathe without feeling pain or anxiety in her chest.

Then she thought about the ranch and all the men who worked there. Instantly, she thought about Charlie, Ben, and Wyatt. How could she be attracted to each of them? While Charlie held her in the kitchen, she sought out Wyatt's touch. All the while, she thought about Ben and wondered where he was. It was strange and yet natural.

She was desperate for attention. Still, after everything that happened to her and after the most important man in her life deserted her and pushed her away, she still sought love and affection. *What the hell is wrong with me? Didn't getting beaten and nearly forced into prostitution shove reality in my face? The hope of finding happiness and belonging to a family was a childhood dream. The dream is dead.*

No…there was no way she could open herself up for disappointment and betrayal. Never again.

She glanced toward Stacy, feeling envious and rather jealous. Stacy not only had a home and a family but two men who adored her and loved her. The way Eric and Max looked at Stacy brought tears of joy to Anna's eyes. She wished for nothing but happiness for her best friend. She just wished she could be on the receiving end for once in her own life.

Stacy was beautiful both outside and inside. With her short raven red hair and big green eyes, she was stunning. She had always been there for Anna as early as elementary school.

They never lost touch, no matter how many miles stood between them. Texas was a long way from New York, but they still spoke on the phone once a week, or at least no longer than two weeks apart. Her calls perked Anna up and made life bearable.

Max and Eric were lucky.

"Whatcha thinking about over there?" Stacy inquired, drawing Anna's attention toward her.

"How lucky I am to have a best friend like you and how lucky Eric and Max are."

Stacy smiled.

"I'm lucky to have you, and I'm blessed to have found true love, double style," Stacy stated with a bit of a Texas drawl.

Anna laughed.

"I couldn't imagine one love, never mind two simultaneously."

"Oh, come on, Anna, you're gorgeous. I've seen the way the men around here have been eyeing you. You'll be going out on dates and being the hottest item in town in no time."

Anna laughed.

"Sorry, Stacy, but that's not me at all. I'm quiet, shy, and picky."

"Is that so? I find it hard to believe that you didn't date a bunch back in New York. I always wondered when I would get that call saying you were in love."

Anna looked toward the water and sighed.

"No time for dating, working double shifts every day and night."

Stacy sighed.

"Well, no need to worry about that now. You're in Texas, and you don't have to work double shifts."

"I will need to find work, though, and if there's nothing in Pearl, it's more the reason to move on."

"You'll find something if you want to. I know the restaurant is hiring. You always loved cooking, maybe the owner has some available shifts for a cook."

"That might work."

"As far as the dating thing, I'm not pushing you, Anna. Things have a way of working themselves out."

"I know. I'm too scared right now for that. Men make me nervous, and after New York, I don't know when I'll get over that fear."

"You seem to be comfortable with Wyatt, Charlie, and Ben." Stacy smiled, then sat back in her chair.

Anna felt her cheeks warm.

"They've been very kind to me. I know it's because they feel sorry for me. They've been real hospitable."

"Hospitable, my ass! Those three are interested in you."

Anna sat up in her chair and grabbed the armrests.

"What?"

"Either you're lying to me about noticing, or you really are clueless when it comes to men."

"The latter, I'm afraid. I've never had time for boys or men. It's always been about taking care of dad and covering medical bills while mom was still alive. There was never time for me, and life just passed me by. Here I am, the twenty-three-year-old virgin."

"Virgin!" Stacy jumped out of her chair and nearly stumbled and fell.

Quickly, she recovered and placed her hands on her hips.

"Start talking now, girl!"

Anna cringed. She felt so embarrassed for shouting that out, but it was true, and Stacy got her all fired up about men and dating.

"I'm afraid it's true. I don't know a thing about sex or men or any of the signs."

"Oh, darling, that is nothing to be ashamed of. I wish I hadn't slept with Alex back in college. I could have given Eric and Max something sacred and special. You still have a chance to find true love and embrace it fully, with every part of you."

Now Anna stood up.

"Me? In love with a man? Not gonna happen, Stacy."

"Why the hell not?"

"Too much fucking baggage, damn it!" Now Anna was annoyed.

Stacy covered her mouth with her hand and laughed.

"What?" Anna demanded to know what was so funny.

"I don't think I have ever heard you curse, never mind use the word fuck."

Anna stuck out her tongue.

"Very funny. Thanks a lot."

"Okay, little virgin, let's discuss this in more detail. I have got to hear your reasoning behind remaining a virgin and never finding true love."

Anna took a deep breath and began using her fingers to count off all the reasons she should remain single.

"One, I've always been the breadwinner and have worked my ass off all these years despite any stereotypical and chauvinistic barriers along the way. Men don't find that type of independence easy to handle. They want to be in charge, and a man in charge is a man with the power to hurt and cause pain."

Stacy swallowed hard. "That's just bullshit. Real men love independent women. The difference between the men you're used to and men I know is they actually care. If a man loves his woman, he can accept her need to be independent and can encourage her to live her life to the fullest just like him. Go on, give me another one."

"Two!" Anna raised her voice.

"Men need to dominate and control and…cause pain." Anna began to cry.

Immediately, Stacy pulled her into an embrace.

"Oh, Anna. You just haven't met men who would cherish you and love you and never bring harm to you."

"They don't exist," Anna cried, then laughed at how childish the words sounded to her own ears.

"Sure they do. Look at Eric and Max. Never mind Charlie, Wyatt, and Ben."

Anna pulled away. "No, no, no, can't you see what I mean? It's not Eric, Max, or the others…it's me. The problem is always going to be with me. I'm scared, Stacy. I'm so damn scared. I can't sleep, I can't…live a normal life. I feel like I'm destined for pain. Like I'm no one, and I'm stumbling through life taking up space."

"No, Anna, it's not true. Don't think that way."

"I couldn't even see what my own father was doing."

Anna crossed her arms in front of her chest and rubbed her arms. She looked out across the water, and Stacy stood beside her.

"I should have demanded that he show me receipts for the shopping, for the rent, for the bills. But I was afraid. I was afraid of being alone, and I was afraid of his drunken stupor."

"He was abusive, Anna?"

"Yes…he didn't hit me as often as when I was a kid or when momma was dying, but he had some bad nights."

Stacy cursed under her breath and caressed Anna's shoulders.

"When he didn't pay the rent after I gave him the money and the landlord threatened to evict us, I should have demanded he straighten out. I was working every day and every night, getting four hours of sleep, while he drank. I should have known something was up that night I arrived home so late and he wasn't there."

Anna began to shake.

* * * *

Stacy felt her own throat tighten and the tears begin to form in her eyes. She had to be strong for Anna. Anna needed to tell her what happened.

"What happened?"

"When I got home, I was thinking how crappy our apartment complex was and how there was no security and garbage everywhere. I was tired. I had been working so much to make up the money for the back rent. As soon as I saw that the door was unlocked, I should have run back downstairs."

"Instead, I figured my dad was drunk again and forgot to lock the door. I thought for sure I would have found him on the couch, passed out or even on the bathroom floor. But as I entered and tossed my purse on the couch, there was no sign of him."

Anna inhaled, and Stacy waited for her to continue. She felt Anna's body tense, and then her voice began to quiver.

"I never saw them. Not until the one guy grabbed me and the other emerged from my bedroom."

"Who were they?"

"Men my dad owed money to. They had warned him that time was up and the money was due and now they were going to send a clear message. Pay up, or your daughter gets the punishment."

"Oh, my god, Anna, what did you do?"

"I tried to run. I tried to explain that I didn't know where my father was, but they didn't believe me. They touched me and threatened me."

Anna began to cry. "He squeezed my breast so hard. I felt the bruises instantly, his breath against my neck, the smell of his cologne. I can smell it at night…when I'm sleeping," she cried.

Stacy could no longer hide her tears as she held Anna.

"They started hitting me, demanding for me to tell my father that his time was up. I fell to the floor in the fetal position, hoping to block any further hits to my head and face. If I fell unconscious, then I was as good as dead.

"I thought they were going to kill me. The pain was so terrible, and they wouldn't stop kicking me and punching me. Then I heard my father's voice.

"I was so...I was so relieved." She sobbed as Stacy caressed her back.

"What did he do? Did he fight them? Did he have the money?"

"He owed thirty thousand. He didn't have anything."

"What happened?"

"He told them that he didn't have the money and that he needed more time. They told him he was out of time and that they would take me...take me as down payment."

"What?"

"I cried for him to help me, but the other man kept fondling me, touching me everywhere. I didn't want him to rape me, Stacy. I didn't want to go with them."

"I know, honey. I understand. What did you do?"

"As the guys continued to touch me and talk about my body and turning me...and turning me into a cash machine...my father asked if anyone needed a drink."

"What the fuck!"

"I couldn't believe it. I was so helpless. I was in so much pain I could hardly stand, and the guy kept touching me. God, Stacy, I can feel his hands on me. When I look in the mirror and see the bruises, I can picture him there."

Anna cried and tried to control her breathing. Stacy cried as well, feeling such hatred and anger toward Anna's father, she wished she could kill him herself.

"They told him they were taking me to whore me out to get back the cash he owed. I pleaded for my dad to help. He told them...he told them...to take me. That he didn't care, that I meant nothing to him." Anna couldn't stop crying.

"The slimy bastard! How could he do that?" Stacy cried.

She pulled Anna into an embrace, and they held one another tight.

A few minutes passed before Anna calmed her breathing, pulled away, and continued.

"I had to get out of there. I couldn't let them take me away."

"What did you do? How did you escape?" Stacy cried along with Anna.

"I told them I had money stashed in my room. I said I would give them the money I had and that I would get the rest of the money my dad owed them as soon as I could. They believed me, but when they asked how much, and I told them a few thousand…" Anna paused. The tears began to streak down her cheeks as she locked gazes with Stacy.

"Yes?" Stacy asked.

"My father called me a bitch and hit me."

Stacy covered her mouth with her hand in shock. *No wonder she's so scared. How could she ever trust anyone again?*

"I knew he didn't love me. It was the final straw. He was going to let them take me. He only cared about the money I made and supporting him. There was no love there.

"I quickly headed into my room, closed the door, and prayed they didn't follow me. The one guy wanted to break me in. I was afraid he was going to do it right there in the bedroom while my father and the other guy stood outside the door. I grabbed the money I had left and climbed out the window. By the grace of god, I climbed the fire escape and jumped the last twelve feet or so. I ran until I caught a cab and headed to the airport. You know the rest."

Stacy took Anna's hand and squeezed it.

"I love you so much, Anna. I'm so sorry that he hurt you and that those men hurt you. I promise that you'll be safe here. I know the men will protect you. You don't have to run anymore."

Anna wiped the tears from her eyes and held her ribs.

"I don't know if the men will try to find me. They were dead set on making me theirs. They were very evil, very bad men. My father obviously can't be trusted, and he could give them your address or name. I can't bring this to your home. I won't put you in danger, Stacy."

"Nonsense! These are Texas cowboys, and they're a helluva lot tougher than any city gangsters or thugs. Plus, Wyatt is a real badass, never mind my Max and the others. Wyatt has connections in New York, and Charlie was in the Marines. You can't get better protection than that."

"I don't feel right coming here and interrupting their lives, Stacy. They don't have to fight my battles. Someone could get hurt."

"Why don't we let the men make their own decision?"

Anna shook her head. Stacy held her hand and wouldn't release it.

"They'll need to know the truth. They'll want to be prepared just in case those guys come looking."

Anna turned toward the water.

"They'll hate me."

"I doubt that very much." Stacy giggled.

"What?" Anna asked.

"It's getting late, and we're gonna have to start getting dinner ready for the men. I'll talk to them tonight. Don't be surprised if Charlie, Wyatt, or Ben are there and want to tuck you in."

"Tuck me in?" Anna asked as Stacy began to gather up their stuff.

"Don't fret about it now. It will be all right."

Stacy winked, and Anna helped her clean everything up.

As they headed toward the house, they walked side by side talking about their plans to swim in the river once the summer temperatures hit.

Chapter 7

There was silence as Stacy told the men what had happened to Anna back in New York. She tried her hardest not to cry, but the pain and the sadness she felt for her best friend was too powerful to fight.

Eric and Max sat on either side of her for moral support as she retold the story in detail.

"Jesus!" Ben exclaimed as he shook his head and ran his fingers through his hair.

Stacy saw the concern and the anger on the three Cantrell brothers' faces. They were good men, genuine men of great moral fiber, so she expected no less of a response.

"Her own father gave her up knowing that these men would whore her out to make back money he owed, and he did nothing. He said that she meant nothing to him and to take her."

Mumbled curses spread through the room.

Tears streamed down Stacy's cheeks. "Then, when Anna offered what money she had stashed to the men to let her go, her father called her a bitch and struck her as well."

"That bastard!" Ben stated as Wyatt stood and paced the room. He looked like a caged animal.

"How did she escape, Stace?" Charlie asked.

"She climbed out the window and down the fire escape. She grabbed a cab, then headed to the airport and straight here in all that pain."

"My God! It's a miracle she's even alive," Charlie added.

"She was running on pure adrenaline. She was running for her life," Wyatt whispered as he looked toward the empty doorway and the hall as if he could see Anna sleeping in the bedroom upstairs.

"She's safe and sound asleep. Doc Jones gave her something to help her sleep better because of the nightmares," Stacy added as she held Eric's hand. Max kept his hand on her knee and caressed her thigh as she told Anna's story.

"She told you everything today by the river?" Charlie asked.

Stacy nodded.

She glanced toward the screened porch and the direction of the river. It was dark outside, and all she could hear was the crickets.

"She was so quiet. She said she felt as if she could finally breathe without feeling anxious or worried about looking over her shoulder. She expressed her fears of men, of being controlled." The men listened to her every word, and she was grateful. Especially if her gut was right and Charlie, Wyatt, and Ben were interested in Anna.

"It's important that you understand something. All of you," Stacy whispered as she took a moment to lock gazes with the three men before her.

"She feels defeated, unsure, and intimidated. Her experience with men that have entered her life has been of abuse, neglect, and control. She's twenty-three, she's had to financially support her family, care for her mom until she died and support her father, pay the regular bills and medical bills. She's never been taken care of." Stacy swallowed hard, then began to cry.

"On the walk back from the river, she said…she said the only love she ever had that she could count on was…was…my friendship." Stacy felt Eric wrap his arms around her shoulders.

"It's okay, honey. You're a great friend," Eric whispered. Max squeezed her knee.

"She never let on to the abuse all these years. Sure, I knew he hit her a few times when she was younger but not during adulthood. I didn't know that her father continued to treat her like this. She never told me."

"How could you know? You hadn't seen her in so long. There's only so much you can detect over a phone, baby. She's a fighter, Stacy. What good would it have been to tell you?" Max asked.

"Maybe I could have gone to see her. Maybe I could have made her leave there and come with me."

"She wouldn't have left, Stacy. From what you've told us, it's obvious that she's not a quitter. She sees things through, no matter how tough. She wanted her father's love, and she thought by taking care of him, supporting him, and working so hard that she would get that love from him," Charlie responded.

The room went silent, and Stacy leaned into Eric more as he held her.

Wyatt exhaled. "What we need to do now is get as much information from Anna as possible. I can make some calls, discretely, of course, and decide the best way to handle an investigation. Max and I will come up with a plan, and if we can get a description of these men, then we can be sure to get those photos out to the community. Any strangers come into town, we'll know immediately," Wyatt stated.

"She knows that you were going to tell us, Stacy?" Ben asked.

"Yes. She's most concerned about me. She wants to leave here, guys. She wants to stay on the run and keep any trouble away from us. She expressed concern over all our well-being."

"That's crazy! She's the one that needs the protection. What could she possibly be thinking? She's a little thing. How could she protect herself out there on the streets?" Wyatt exclaimed. His hardened expression was traditional bossy Wyatt.

"Her sole concern is about Stacy and all of us. Her own safety isn't even a thought," Max added.

"Well, that's gonna change."

Everyone looked toward Charlie.

He raised his eyebrow in challenge.

"I agree with Charlie. She needs us," Ben added.

Stacy yawned.

"You should get to bed, honey. It's real late," Max whispered to her, and Eric kissed her on the head before she stood up.

She held their gazes and squeezed their hands.

"I know she'll be safe here." She looked toward the others. "Please take things slow with her, guys. She's not experienced, and she's real fragile right now," Stacy stated, and before they could respond, she headed out of the room.

* * * *

Charlie felt such heaviness in his chest. One look at Ben and Wyatt and he knew they felt the same way. In fact, Wyatt looked like he wanted to hit something. If they were going to make Anna feel safe, he was going to have to control his anger and his temper. Wyatt tended to be controlling, authoritative, and downright mean sometimes. Being the sheriff, he was always in a state of authority, so no one dared mess around in town.

When he thought about Anna and her concern over them, he admired her strength and independence. She was a good person and a great friend to Stacy. These were characteristics he liked in a woman but had yet to meet until Anna. Knowing his brothers, they would probably agree.

Eric and Max said good night and walked them to the door. Charlie, Ben, and Wyatt walked across the yard to their own house.

Wyatt stopped and looked up toward the bedroom window where Anna slept.

"I wish I could see her. Just make sure that she's sound asleep and feeling okay," he said as he stood watching.

"I know what you mean," Ben replied.

"Yeah, she felt real good in my arms the other night," Charlie whispered as he looked up toward the window as well.

"What? You slept in the bed with her?" Wyatt asked, sounding angry.

"She had the nightmare, and I helped her calm down. She clung to me, and I stayed with her. She's beautiful."

"I'm gonna find the bastards that did this to her so she doesn't have to be afraid."

Charlie looked at Wyatt then at Ben.

"We want in on this. Anything you find out, you let us know, and if we have to head to New York, we'll do it."

Wyatt locked gazes with Charlie and Ben.

They all nodded in agreement.

"What are we agreeing to here that we're not stating?" Ben asked.

They were silent a moment until Charlie spoke.

"I want her. I want to love her, take care of her, and show her how wonderful life can be after feeling such heartache and pain. I know what it's like. I thought the war had destroyed my heart and my soul. But if it weren't for you two, for Eric and Max, or the Triple C ranch, I'd have ended my life."

Ben placed his hand on Charlie's shoulder. "Those were tough times. We made it through together, and we'll help Anna make it through this."

"I always knew we would find a woman that we could share. Each of us has many things to offer Anna if she'll accept us," Wyatt replied.

"That's going to be the fun part," Ben exclaimed. Both Charlie and Wyatt looked at him funny.

"Wooing our woman, fellas…She's stunning, she's petite, and, damn, can she cook."

Wyatt and Charlie laughed.

"That isn't going to be so easy to do. We all have pretty intense personalities," Charlie replied.

"As long as we're on the same page, we'll handle this together," Ben added as he took the front porch steps two at a time.

Wyatt glanced at the bedroom window one more time.

Charlie exhaled, feeling the same anxiety he was sure that Wyatt felt.

"We don't know that much about her," Wyatt whispered, and Charlie sensed his brother's hesitation.

"No, we don't. But we'll work on that. We'll each take time to get to know her and see if she really is the one for us."

"Charlie, she's been through a lot. I'm rough around the edges and then some."

Charlie leaned against the railing to the steps.

"What are you afraid of?"

"I don't pussyfoot around people, male or female. I'm straightforward, and if I want something, I go get it."

"What are you not saying?"

Charlie watched Wyatt run his fingers through his hair.

"I don't know if I can be gentle, and I don't want to hurt her. She's been hurt, and she seems like a genuinely good person. Her concern over Stacy and all of us before her own safety and well-being is a perfect example of her selflessness. You and Ben are good at the coddling stuff, not me. I just don't think a ménage relationship with her will work."

"That's crazy thinking. You're just scared because you are attracted to her, you admire her character and her good looks."

"I didn't say I was scared." Wyatt pushed away from the post and walked up the stairs as if ending the conversation.

Charlie stopped him by touching his shoulder.

"There's no need to rush this. She may not even be interested in us or ever have considered a ménage relationship. It's going to be new for all of us, so let's just focus on making her feel safe and making her want to remain on Triple C."

Wyatt released a sigh instead of giving an answer as he walked into the house.

* * * *

A week had passed, and Anna was feeling more comfortable with everyone on the Triple C. Especially Ben, Charlie, and Wyatt.

She had enjoyed a stroll along the walkway and gardens, meeting Ben along the way.

"Hi."

"Hi." Anna returned the greeting as Ben stopped to speak with her. She was sitting on a bench where three initials were etched inside a heart. She had been tracing the letters when Ben arrived.

"How are you feeling today?" Ben asked as he placed his hands in his front pockets.

"Good, thank you. I was just enjoying the gardens again. I love how the flowers are growing so full and beautiful already."

She watched as Ben looked around them, absorbing her description and agreeing. "You can cut some flowers if you want to."

"Oh, really?" She sat forward on the bench and glanced around.

"There are cutters and a basket by the shed out front. My mom used to pick flowers all the time."

Anna smiled in response.

"Matter of fact, that heart with the three sets of initials on the bench is my parents'." He pointed to the bench, and Anna glanced at the initials she had traced earlier.

She realized that there were three sets. Two wives and one husband or two husbands and one wife? The thought stirred something inside her.

"Our dads made sure they kept this garden beautiful for our mom. She loved picking flowers."

She wasn't quite sure how to respond. She had never been exposed to multiple partners and sharing in a relationship. Not until her phone call from Stacy and her best friend meeting Eric and Max.

Stacy had said the town had many families just like theirs.

Anna had yet to go to town again, but now that Stacy got her an interview for tomorrow with the restaurant, she would have to take notice.

"You look real pretty today, Anna. I like your hair down."

"Thank you. So where were you off to?' she asked, trying to avoid the awkward and more intimate subjects for a conversation. Ben made her nervous. All the Cantrells did.

Ben had a look about him. He was very outgoing and attractive, and he knew it. Not that he walked around saying "I'm hot" or anything like that, he just had a star quality about him. It made her smile.

"I was heading to the stables to check on some newborn colts. Do you want to come along?" He reached his hand out for her to take it.

She took a deep breath and carefully reached for his hand. When they touched, she felt the instant attraction.

He smiled as he held her hand and led her toward the stables.

* * * *

"Come over here, Anna. You have to see this," Ben exclaimed, pulling her along with him through the stables.

They came to a stall that had a large horse Anna guessed was the mother and a newborn colt. It was wobbling on shaky legs and fell a few times. Anna covered her mouth.

She felt a hand on her shoulder and tensed a moment until she realized it was Ben's.

"It's okay. He was only born about an hour ago."

"That's amazing!" Anna watched as the mother licked her baby's fur and then nudged it to continue to try and succeed in standing and walking.

"It's beautiful to watch, isn't it?"

Anna turned toward Charlie's voice behind her.

He looked handsome today, as usual, in his forest green checkered shirt and dark blue jeans. His hat had hay on it, along with his shirt.

Quickly, she turned away and back toward the sight in front of her.

These men were so lucky to be able to witness this all the time. It was touching to see the mom guiding and protecting the colt. It made Anna feel good to have witnessed it.

"Were you in the garden today?" Charlie asked, and both Anna and Ben turned their attention towards him.

She nodded.

"Did you pick any flowers?"

"No," she replied then wrung her fingers together in front of her. Being in such an enclosed place with both Charlie and Ben made her fidget.

"Well, next time, bring along a basket and some clippers to take some flowers. That's why we planted them and continue to grow so many. Did Ben show you the bench?"

"She was sitting there when I found her."

Charlie smiled.

"Our mom used to sit out there and enjoy the garden before she picked her flowers. Our dads told us she was the one who carved their initials in the wood."

"That's nice. The garden is lovely. Next time I will pick some if you're sure it's okay?"

"Definitely," Ben replied.

They stared at her a few moments, and she felt awkward. It was hard enough to breathe and not stumble through her words, let alone maintain a conversation. Both men were so appealing.

Before she made a fool of herself, she made an excuse and headed back toward the house.

* * * *

"What did you think?" Ben asked.

"I think she's sweet."

"But timid."

"You'd be, too, if you survived what she has. I'm glad you had a chance to spend some time with her. She seemed comfortable with you."

"She did, and I was glad that I found her in the gardens. I was worried when Stacy said she hadn't seen her."

"Well, as long as she stays on the ranch, we can keep an eye on her. I'm glad she's finally talking to us more."

"Me, too," Ben replied then walked over to the corral to take another look at the colt.

* * * *

Anna borrowed a dress from Stacy. She knew she needed to impress the owner of Francine's Restaurant if she wanted a job there. Stacy helped her with a fancy updo, and she gave her some makeup and lip gloss.

"Now, Jack is a flirt and a half, but he's harmless. His wife, Mary, is a sweetheart, and as long as you work hard, respect their orders, and show them respect, you should be fine. Once they try your cooking, they won't want to let you go. So, be confident," Stacy told her before they left the room and headed downstairs.

When they arrived in the kitchen, the whistles and comments began.

Anna froze in place and lowered her head.

"Hot damn, woman, you are a sight!" Ben exclaimed as he approached her, took her in his arms, and twirled her around.

Anna grabbed a hold of him and laughed at his response. When he finally set her down, he held her in his arms and locked gazes with her.

"You're beautiful," he whispered then kissed her cheek.

"Let me get a look at her, you hog!" Charlie exclaimed, pulling her out of Ben's arms and into his own. He held her at arm's length and slowly took in the sight of her from head to toe. "Stunning, Anna. Absolutely stunning," he whispered then kissed her lips softly and so quickly she didn't have time to let his action sink in.

"Give the woman some room. We have to leave now," Stacy exclaimed, grabbing Anna by her hand and pulling her out the door.

* * * *

They headed into town, and Anna touched her fingers to her lips. She felt her cheeks burn, and her stomach quivered.

"What's wrong, y'all feeling nervous about the interview?" Stacy asked as she exited the Triple C Ranch.

"What the hell just happened back there?" Anna whispered, still caressing her lips and feeling Charlie's touch. Ben had kissed her as well, and she was shocked.

Stacy looked over her shoulder and pretended she didn't understand, but Anna knew she did.

"Don't play dumb with me. You saw them back there. Ben and Charlie…"

"Kissed you. So what? Didn't you like it?"

"Stacy?"

"Oh, come on, Anna. I know you're a virgin in the bedroom, but a woman's intuition should be kicking in. They're hot for you, and so is Wyatt."

"Wyatt?" Anna felt her insides coil up tight, and her hands began to sweat. She was having trouble breathing and wondered if this was a panic attack. She figured at some point she would have a nervous breakdown. Why now? Why on the way to the potential job. She needed this. She needed to make money to buy clothes, to find a place to live.

She lost all focus as she felt the truck stop and Stacy grab her hand.

"Calm down, honey. Just relax and breathe. Little breaths then release." Stacy kept talking to her until finally Anna was breathing normally.

Her eyes filled up with tears.

"I can't do this."

"Yes, you can, honey. You're going to grab that inner strength of yours, put on your tough girl confident face, and land you a job. Then you're going to take things slow with the men. I've already had Eric and Max talk to them. They know to take things slow."

"A talk with them? About me? Why?" Anna asked, feeling the panic attack begin again.

"Calm down, and just focus on the job. The men won't hurt you, honey. They were attracted to you immediately. The more that they're around you, the more their attraction grows."

"Oh, my Lord. They're so…they're so big and gorgeous and older. Much older than I am. They could have their pick of women. Look around you," Anna exclaimed, encompassing the town with a hand gesture.

"Nonsense. They want you. Now hush up and fix your eyes. I'll introduce you to Mary and Jack then, when you're done, you can meet me at Doc Jones's office."

"You didn't say that you had an appointment."

"I didn't want the men to fuss. They would get all serious and wind up following me here. No worries. Everything is fine."

Anna fixed her lip gloss and eyes then exited the truck. This was it. It was time to take control of her life, her destiny, and make a new start.

* * * *

"There's no time like the present, doll. Why don't ya show us what ya got?" Jack Boslow, the owner, stated as he crossed his arms over his large chest. His wife, Mary, gave Anna a wink before she stepped out of the kitchen to seat more people for lunch.

Ann looked around at the unfriendly faces, taking notice that they were all men. No problem for her. She was used to running a kitchen. Male or female, as long as they did their job, it was fine with her.

"What's your favorite dish?" she asked Jack as she grabbed an apron and washed her hands by the sink. Lunch orders were being called out around her.

Jack eyed her suspiciously, then said, "Let's start off real simple. I want to see what a New York cook can do with my chicken salad."

Anna smiled then quickly went in search of ingredients she could use. While she did it, she introduced herself to other staff in the kitchen and thanked them for the stuff she took.

Before long, she was chopping, dicing, sprinkling, and combining what she could find to make a gourmet chicken salad. "Are you allergic to anything?"

A nod of his head was all she got, so she began to add the chopped grapes, the diced walnuts, and chopped cranberries. Next, she added a little bit of mayo mixed with a tad bit of horseradish sauce and a few spices.

She toasted some thick-sliced Italian bread and seasoned it with some more stuff before placing it on the plate. She topped the bread with her chicken salad concoction, added the top slice, then cut it in half. She then added a fresh strawberry on top of each slice. To the side, she added pickles and Francine's famous fries.

She handed the plate to Jack just as his wife entered.

Anna waited as Jack eyed the dish, as if concerned that the food might kill him.

"I'm not a fruit kind of guy," he stated.

"Doc Jones said you need more fruit in your diet. Now, try the damn thing then move over so I can have some."

Anna hid a smile at Mary's tone.

Jack took a bite then chewed. He made some humming noises then took another bite. He closed his eyes and continued to eat as Mary took a bite of the second half.

"This is delicious! What did you do to my chicken salad, girl?" Francine asked as Jack picked the scraps off the plate.

"Just a little New York-style chicken salad like the man asked," Anna teased, and Mary laughed.

"Well, Jack?"

"What?"

"If you don't hire her right now, then I will," Mary stated, and Jack laughed.

"When can ya start, honey?"

"Tomorrow good?" Anna asked.

"Right now would be great, but I guess that's too much to ask. Be here by nine in the morning for prep and to get the kitchen staff ready for whatever you need."

"Hey, Miguel!" Jack called to the current cook.

"*Sí, señor?*"

"You're off the hook starting tomorrow. We got ourselves a real New York chef right here."

Anna felt terrible. She didn't want the other man to lose his job.

"Jack, Mary...I don't want to take his job away. I thought you were in need of a cook?"

"Oh, don't fret, honey. Miguel has been dying to quit being in charge. He's only been at it for a few weeks after Chuck the old cook took off for Vegas and never came back."

"*Señorita…gracias*," Miguel added as he kissed Anna's hand and went back to work.

Anna looked around at the now-smiling faces. She wasn't too sure what to think, but at least she had a job. The pay was pretty good, too.

She thanked the Boslows then headed out of the kitchen. While Jack showed her the front of the place, some young men made a few comments and began flirting with her. Jack and Mary introduced her as the new cook.

"When ya startin', honey?" one real nice-looking cowboy asked as he eyed her from head to toe.

She smiled softly as she took in the other patrons. The men seemed to outnumber the women in this town, and they all seemed to be in pairs or in threes. She swallowed the lump in her throat and thought about Charlie, Ben, and Wyatt.

"She'll be starting tomorrow, so you fellas be sure to stop by and let us know what ya think of her cooking," Jack stated.

"What's your name, good looking?" someone else asked, and Anna began to get nervous. There were a lot of men in this town, and the way they eyed her made her anxious to leave. Each of them was attractive and what the waitresses back in New York would have called delicious eye candy. She felt herself blush at their continued compliments.

"The name is Anna, and she's stayin' at the Triple C." Everyone turned toward the deep, authoritative voice. Anna swallowed hard at the sight of Wyatt standing in the doorway in his sheriff's uniform. Men cleared their throats and went back to eating lunch as he made his way toward her. The closer he got, the farther up she had to look.

He wrapped his arm around her waist and pulled her to him. She gasped at his show of possession, but everyone else seemed to go about their business. Out of all three brothers, he had been the quietest around her. Small conversations here and there were about all they shared. She had wondered if he even liked her. Unlike Ben and

Charlie, Wyatt didn't let his feelings show. If anything, he seemed to keep his distance from her.

When Wyatt reached up and touched her cheek, she closed her eyes and absorbed the feel of his embrace.

"So ya got yourself a job, huh, honey?" he asked.

"Yes…as the cook."

He raised his eyebrows and then looked over at Jack.

"You take good care of our Anna, Jack. I expect you all will be real happy with her cooking."

"That I will, Jack. You betcha."

Anna wondered who he meant when he said *our* Anna.

Immediately, she thought about Charlie and Ben. Suddenly, she couldn't wait to share the news with them. How silly of her. They weren't her boyfriends. Did she want them to be? Did they think she was interested? *Am I?*

She felt Wyatt release his hold but not completely as he tipped his hat good day to everyone and escorted her out of the restaurant.

* * * *

Once they were outside, he took her hand and brought it to his lips. He kissed her knuckles, and all she could do was stare at him in awe.

The sheriff was a perfect specimen of a man and the stereotypical looking sheriff aside from his young age. He had large, strong hands and an aura around him.

He looked her over. "You look real pretty today, Anna."

She glanced at her outfit. "It's Stacy's. I borrowed it," she whispered and wondered why she sounded like she lost her voice.

* * * *

Wyatt felt the tightness in his chest. The way she looked, the way she sounded right now, made his cock throb and his stomach quiver. He was having a difficult time keeping conversations with her simple back at the ranch. He was still determining whether or not Anna was the one for him and his brothers. The more he spoke to her or heard about the conversations she had with his brothers, the more interested he became.

He got so jealous back there at Francine's at the way the men gawked at her. He knew what they were thinking. Hell, he heard a few men comment about her body. He had to stake a claim and make his and his brothers' intentions known. It's not like the Cantrells were the only family in town that was involved in ménage relationships. The town was known for it.

He leaned over and gave Anna a quick, soft kiss on the lips. It was torture to not taste more of her, but he was the sheriff, and he was standing in the middle of town.

* * * *

Anna held on to Wyatt's forearms as he released her lips. Her eyes remained closed a moment, and she felt embarrassed when she opened them to find him smirking at her.

She must seem so naive to him. The idea that all three of them had touched her and kissed her today was unnerving to say the least. It just wasn't possible to be attracted to three men at once, never mind normal. *Haven't I learned my lesson about giving away my heart?*

She sobered instantly as thoughts of sadness nearly overwhelmed her. She turned away in his arms and made an attempt to escape. She had gotten only two steps before a strong arm came around her waist from behind, bringing her back up against Wyatt's solid chest.

"Whoa there, honey, slow down. I'm not going to hurt you," he whispered from way above her head. His size, his potential strength, and his uniform made her body shake.

Wyatt used his free hand to caress her arm and shoulder. She felt every move, every sensation of his touch. Then he tilted her chin sideways as he leaned over with his face near her shoulder.

"I didn't mean to scare you, doll. I just couldn't resist tasting those sexy lips of yours. You look so damn edible."

She tried to shy away and look down, but he pulled her tighter against him. The feel of his manhood against her back and iron thighs against the material of her skirt had her breathing heavy and feeling faint.

"You feeling all right, sweetie? You look like you're about to faint," he said, full of concern. Then he turned her toward him and pulled her into an embrace against his chest.

He was silent, as if waiting for her to say something. She couldn't think a coherent thought. She felt frazzled, turned on, and she shouldn't. It wasn't right to have these feelings for three men, never mind brothers.

"I…please don't do that again," she whispered, and her voice cracked.

Wyatt scrunched his eyebrows together and looked downright mad.

"Don't do what?" he asked, although he knew precisely what she meant.

He stared down at her, holding her gaze, and she could see the mischief in his eyes.

"Kiss me."

"My pleasure," he stated then kissed her again.

It wasn't what she meant. She wanted him not to kiss her but…now that he was, it felt so good and so right.

The sound of someone clearing his throat pulled her from her daze. "Sheriff," some older couple passing by said, and Wyatt tipped his hat and said good afternoon to them, never releasing his hold on Anna.

"That was real nice, Anna. You can ask me for a kiss anytime you want," he teased then caressed her lip with his thumb.

"No. I didn't mean for you to kiss me again. I meant, don't kiss me ever again," she stated in a huff, turning away from him.

"Didn't you like it?" he asked, pulling her closer against his chest, then he winked.

"Please…I…I don't want to cause any trouble," she stated, hoping that she could deflect what was really bothering her about this.

The sheriff looked around them, and Anna followed his line of sight. It seemed they were drawing quite the amount of attention in town.

"I need to go…Stacy is waiting for me."

She stepped away, only to be pulled back by Wyatt.

"One thing, darling, before you go. We'll talk about this later." He leaned down and kissed her quickly and softly before releasing her.

Anna pulled away then looked both ways before she crossed the street toward the doctor's office.

* * * *

Stacy was awfully quiet when they got into the truck to head toward the ranch.

"So, is everything all right? What did the doctor say?" Anna asked.

"Everything is fine. It's just as I expected," Stacy replied as she continued to drive out of town.

"Well? Is it anything serious? Do you need to take anything for it?"

Anna waited for Stacy to respond, wondering why she was acting so strange.

"Just some prenatal vitamins," Stacy replied, and Anna immediately turned toward her.

"Say that again?"

Stacy smiled wide. "I'm pregnant."

"Oh, my God! That is so awesome! The guys are going to be so thrilled." Anna began to cry, and so did Stacy.

"Oh, Anna, I'm so glad that you're happy about this. I was afraid that you wouldn't be."

"Me? What are you, crazy? I love babies. Who in the world wouldn't?"

Stacy wiped her eyes as she drove.

"I can't believe it."

"When are you going to tell Eric and Max?"

"I don't know. I have a feeling that once those two hear the news, they are going to be even more protective than before."

"That's what you want, Stacy. You want them to be so into it and so loving. They're going to make great fathers," Anna said then covered her mouth to try and hide the tears.

Stacy reached over and touched her hand.

"They are going to be great fathers. They will be thrilled."

"I'm so happy for you, Stacy. I think you should do something really romantic with them. Maybe I can stay at the hotel in town tonight."

"Don't be silly. I wouldn't make you leave the house."

"Well, I just thought you might feel a little uncomfortable with me in the house while you have a romantic evening at home with the men."

"Your presence hasn't stopped us from having romantic evenings yet," Stacy added sarcastically.

Anna giggled and blushed before she cleared her throat.

"Don't you sass me, girl. I so don't need to be picturing such activity going on while I'm alone and sleeping on the other side of the house."

"Well, I'm sure if you want to leave the house for the night, you could just mention sleeping over at Wyatt, Ben, and Charlie's place. They would love to have you."

Anna froze in a stunned stare at Stacy.

Stacy laughed as she pulled into the driveway at the Triple C ranch.

As they parked the truck, the men seemed to come out from everywhere.

Eric came out from the stables, along with Ben, and Charlie came around from the other side of the horse training stables. It was as if they waited to hear the sound of the truck arriving.

Anna turned toward Stacy. "You can have the house tonight to tell Eric and Max the good news. I think I'll try that little hotel in town. It looked really nice. I'd love to get the whole town of Pearl experience, really." Anna rambled on and on, and Stacy continued to laugh at her.

"I give you all of about two seconds after telling your men that you're going to a hotel before one of them is tossing you over his shoulder and bringing you to their place to stay. So don't be silly."

"My men? Who would that be?"

"You know damn straight who I'm talking about. Two of them are headed this way, and one had his mouth all over you on Main Street just about twenty minutes ago."

With that, Stacy opened her door and stepped out and into Eric's arms.

"Hey, honey. How did it go? Does Francine's have a new cook?" Eric asked as he led Stacy around to the front of the truck where Ben and Charlie stood with Anna. They had helped her out of the truck and both had a hand on her shoulder.

"Come on, honey, tell us the news," Charlie asked.

"I am the new cook at Francine's starting tomorrow."

They each cheered and gave her a hug, then Charlie pulled her to him and checked her forehead for fever.

"Tomorrow seems kind of soon. Are you sure you're up to it?" he asked, sounding concerned but also controlling. Anna didn't like the feeling she got, but she forced a smile.

"I'll be fine. Plus, I need to make some money. I don't have much left."

Anna felt another hand lay across her back as Ben whispered next to her ear. "We'll take care of you, honey. Any money you need, you just come to us."

Anna swallowed hard. This was getting to be a bit much. She felt smothered at the moment, like everyone was in control of her life except for her.

She took a step away from them and placed some distance between her and Ben and Charlie.

"Listen," she stated, louder than she meant, causing everyone to look at her, including Eric and Stacy.

She took a deep breath and began more calmly.

"Listen, please…I appreciate your kindness. I truly do, but there's no need to patronize me. I'm a grown woman, I've been down and out and then some, so believe me when I tell you that I can handle things. I will not accept money from you. Any of you. I am taking that job and starting tomorrow, so things will get better." Charlie began to object, and Ben looked ready to yell. She stopped them with a raise of her hand palm forward and a stern look.

"I am fine, Charlie. I'm used to being on my own and handling it all, whether I am sick, injured, or just plain exhausted. Now, Stacy has some plans for tonight, and I'm taking a little tour of Pearl for the evening. I'll be staying at the hotel in town with my last fifty bucks. That way, I'll be right in town for my first day at work, and no one will need to drive me there."

Charlie attempted to interrupt again, and this time, Stacy and Max laughed as they quickly removed themselves from the current situation.

Anna wondered what the heck they were doing, and as she watched them go, she felt herself being pulled toward the porch steps of Charlie, Ben, and Wyatt's house.

Charlie sat down on the bench, pulling Anna onto his lap. Ben stood directly in front of them and inches away from Anna.

His arm was gently around her waist, and his other hand lay flat against her thigh.

"What the hell are you talking about?" Charlie asked as Ben stood by with his hands on his hips looking sexy as damn hell. Anna tried not to focus on either man's beauty, but it was pretty hard with her rear plastered on top of rock-solid thighs.

Charlie tilted her chin toward him so he could look into her eyes.

"I think we need to talk about this more calmly. What do you mean you're going to stay in the hotel in town?" Charlie asked.

Anna clasped her fingers together on her lap and began to fidget.

Ben knelt down next to her and Charlie. It was a strange sight, seeing a man Ben's size kneeling down in front of her. His head was level with her chest as he slightly looked up at her. His sandy brown hair tossed around a little with the light spring breeze. He squinted as a strand hit his long eyelashes then smiled at her, noticing she stared. Quickly, Anna looked down toward her hands. Her knuckles were white from gripping them so tightly.

Ben placed his hand over hers.

"Anna, please don't be afraid of us. We're not trying to run your life. We just want to protect you. Now, what's this nonsense about staying in town?"

Anna didn't want to give away Stacy's secret surprise, but the men's response to her statement was intimidating.

"Does Wyatt know?" Charlie asked, and Anna jumped at his statement. For some reason, she feared Wyatt's reaction to her staying in town for the night. Of course, there was the conversation she had with Stacy on the ride over and the way Wyatt kissed her in town and claimed her taken to all the men at the restaurant.

"I...I just need to give Stacy, Max, and Eric some alone time, that's all."

"Then you'll stay with us," Charlie stated.

Anna jumped up off his lap and stood. There was no place to run to because Charlie's legs were in the way, as well as Ben's body.

Charlie held her by her outer thighs, and her legs began to shake. It was an intimate hold for her. Charlie was a big man with large hands that practically covered her whole thigh. With Ben inches away from her back, she felt hot and shaky. She never suffered from claustrophobia, but being sandwiched between these two made her panic.

"No! I can't stay here…No way." Anna crossed her arms in front of her chest.

* * * *

Charlie had to hide his grin from her. She looked so adorable the way she fidgeted with her hands and jumped up off of his lap. She had felt so good sitting there, he nearly lost his ability to speak.

"Anna, it's no big deal. We have two extra bedrooms. You can stay for as long as you like or as long as you think Stacy and the guys need."

"No, I can't. I…I can't…you…you." She shook her head and tried to step by them. Both he and Ben grabbed a hand.

"Whoa there, honey. It's okay," Ben stated, standing in front of her, blocking her path.

Charlie saw the fear in Anna's eyes at being blocked.

"Sit down, Anna. Please?" Charlie asked, and although she hesitated, she took a seat.

"We would never hurt you, Anna. That's something you have to believe and trust about us."

"It's understandable that you're scared, but we would never force ourselves on you. Real men don't do that kind of thing," Ben stated, taking a seat next to her on the swing.

Anna looked shocked at his statement, and Charlie saw the tears reach her eyes.

She looked down at her hands as she spoke.

"I don't know you…either of you."

"Sure you do, doll. You've been around us for a few weeks now. What you see is what you get," Ben stated.

"I wouldn't want you to get the wrong idea. If I stayed…here…I mean."

"No wrong idea. Just us offering an extra bed so you can give Stacy, Max, and Eric some alone time. No strings and no expectations. We just want you to be safe, and staying in town alone is not a good move."

"I would be fine."

"Not a chance we're willing to take," Charlie countered.

"Yeah, especially after what Wyatt said about the men in town asking about you."

"Asking about me? Why?"

Ben and Charlie chuckled.

"Not your worry. Wyatt will spread the word," Charlie added.

"And what word would that be?" Anna asked.

Charlie cupped Anna's chin and tilted it up toward him.

"That you belong to the Cantrell brothers. Wyatt, Ben, and me," Charlie replied, then kissed her long and deep.

By the time he released her lips, she wasn't certain what she just agreed to by spending the weekend in their house.

As Charlie released her, Ben took his turn pulling her toward him and kissing her just as deeply.

She clung to his chest, holding on to the amazing sensations these men sent through her body from their kisses alone. Her mind spun with thoughts of being loved and cherished. But then came reality. As Ben released her lips, she saw the raw desire in his eyes. They wanted her, but was she ready to take such a chance? She feared losing herself and what fraction of an identity she had left. Ben, Charlie, and Wyatt were such different men. She admired their individuality and what she knew about them so far, but intimacy and reacting on emotions wasn't smart thinking. If her present track record was any indication of the possible results, this could prove disastrous. *Me, in a sexual relationship with three men at once? Crazy!*

Chapter 8

Brooklyn, New York

"So you're fucking telling me his kid is so hot that you want to track her down, drag her back here, and use her to make back the money her old man owes us?" Marcus asked.

"He's dead fucking serious. He's had a hard-on for weeks since she skipped town," Jake replied with a snicker.

"Fucking-A, I have. I'm telling you, boss, she's so fucking hot and pure that I might just have to pay her daddy's debt and keep her for myself," Vinny replied.

Marcus laughed. "Son of a bitch! That fucking hot, huh?"

Both Vinny and Jake smiled and nodded their heads.

"Do I get ta give her a whirl when you get back here for letting you leave for a few weeks?"

Vinny looked shocked, but Marcus was the boss, the least he should get besides the thirty grand was a whirl with the woman.

"Only once," Vinny stated, and Marcus laughed.

"What about her old man? Is this going to be a problem?"

"No. He fucking tried to sell her to us for his debt anyway. A real asshole, that one. Meanwhile, she was supposedly working her ass off supporting him and the sick mother before the old lady died. A sad fucking case."

"That does sound sad. Since when did you become a Good fucking Samaritan?" Marcus asked sarcastically.

"Since he felt Anna's big tits and firm, round ass," Jake replied, and they all laughed.

"Where's the deadbeat dad now?" Marcus inquired as he sat behind his desk.

"Dead in a fucking alleyway in the South Bronx," Vinny replied.

"Okay. There's no other family that will come looking for her?"

"Just the one chick she's friends with that the old man told us about. We figured Anna headed there. It's our first stop."

"Okay, then it seems you've got everything covered. Don't leave a mess behind you, and be back here in three weeks. I can't wait to see this Anna," Marcus replied, then chuckled at Jake and Vinny.

* * * *

"I can't believe he wants to try her out, too." Vinny was annoyed.

Jake laughed.

"What the fuck did you expect him to say when you carried on about her? You fucking put a major beating in on her old man. I didn't even get a chance to help you kill him. What the fuck was up with that?"

"He fucking tossed her to us like she was trash."

"How the hell do you know she's not trash?"

"Jake, do you remember her? It was fucking obvious she was an innocent. I think she was a fucking virgin."

"Nooo!"

"Fuck, yes. I want a piece of that, and the more we've learned about her life, the more I want to find her."

"What the fuck for? You don't want to care for her, you want to fuck her and whore her out."

"With her body and looks, she'll make up her old man's debt like that, and then she'll be all mine to fuck whenever I want to."

"What are you going to do, tie her to a bed and leave her there?"

"If I have to. Or she might be so thankful that I saved her from her old man and keeping her after she's used goods that she'll cling to me and serve me in every way."

Jake laughed.

"You are so fucking psycho it's not even funny, Vinny. I think killing people has fucked with your brain."

"Maybe it has, but mark my words, Anna is mine, and no one will stand in my way. If they do, I'll fucking kill them."

"Hey, Marcus said no messes."

"Don't worry, she's in Texas with a bunch of fucking hicks. "Badda bing…badda boom…It will be a piece of cake to knock off anyone in our path and leave them for dead out in a fucking field with vultures and shit."

Jake shook his head.

"I can't believe I'm fucking leaving New York to go to fucking hick, cowboy Texas to find you your whore."

"Believe me, man, we are, and our flight leaves in two days."

* * * *

Anna was walking by the stables when she heard a ruckus going on inside the barn. She watched as a few cowboys walked out looking somber.

"What's going on?" she asked, and the two men looked at her, surprised she was there. They removed their hats and greeted her.

"Sorry, Miss. We didn't see y'all standing there," one of the cowboys stated with a thick accent.

Ben came through the stable doors, and he didn't look happy.

"Anna! What are you doing out here?" he asked, his tone seemed off, as if he was upset that she was there. She lowered her eyes and swallowed hard. It was crazy, but she felt the tears reach her eyes.

"I'm sorry, honey. I didn't mean to sound displeased. We've got a cow in labor, and she just can't seem to deliver on her own. She's having trouble breathing, and it's not looking good."

"Will she lose the calf?" Anna asked.

He nodded.

"Oh, no. Is there anything I can do to help?"

Just then, Charlie called from inside the stable.

Ben turned and headed inside, and Anna did the same, despite the attempts by the other cowboys to stop her.

"Oh, my God!" Anna whispered as she saw the sight.

Charlie was sweating, his hands were covered with blood, and he was trying to assist the cow in delivering her baby. The poor cow was huffing and puffing then it would lay its head down and heave deep, horrible sounding gasps of air.

"Anna, you shouldn't be in here." Ben spoke to her as he helped Charlie.

The sounds were difficult to listen to, and Anna felt terrible for the cow. She had to do something.

Without a second thought, and despite both Ben and Charlie's protests, Anna sat down next to the cow's head and began to caress her fur. She rubbed her chest, recalling doing this many times when her mother was dying and couldn't breathe too well. It had brought her mom some comfort and eventually helped her to calm her breathing and not panic. Although Anna didn't know anything about cows, she thought she would give it a try anyway.

Anna looked down at the cow and her dark brown eyes. She had lifted her head and looked at Anna.

Anna smiled and continued to massage and caress the cow's neck as she spoke to her.

"You need to calm your breathing, lady. You've got a healthy, beautiful baby to deliver, and it's going to need its momma to take care of it. So, come on and breathe for me. Listen to my voice, lady."

Charlie and Ben continued to help the cow.

Time had passed slowly, but Anna refused to give up hope.

"I think it's working, Anna. I think she's trying to push. Keep talking to her," Charlie stated, sounding breathless as he reached inside to help pull the calf out.

"Oh, my God, I don't believe it," Ben said as Charlie pulled the calf while the mother pushed, then mooed really loud. The baby calf was born.

* * * *

"That was amazing, Anna. Absolutely amazing," Ben said as he pulled her into his arms.

Anna laughed as the cow and the calf remained next to one another and Charlie got cleaned up. A few ranch hands came inside to continue to care for the animals and clean up.

Ben caressed her cheek and held her close to him.

"Where did you learn to do that?"

"Do what?" she asked, sounding breathless in Ben's arms.

"Learn to calm a cow down during labor? We thought for sure she wasn't going to make it."

"I had my doubts," Charlie blurted out as he joined them.

Anna shrugged her shoulders.

Ben caressed her lip with his thumb before he leaned forward and kissed her softly. It was a quick kiss but left Anna blushing.

His button-down, blue, plaid shirt sleeve brushed against her neck. He smelled of straw and cologne, and it appealed to her. He was muscular and good looking with his dimples and all.

Charlie took that moment to take her hand into his own and bring it to his lips. The feel of his large hands holding her small hand made her feel protected. He kissed her knuckles as he held her gaze. Her imagination jumped into overdrive as she imagined him taking each digit into his mouth and sucking. She swallowed hard.

Get a grip, woman!

"You're an amazing woman. Thank you for helping."

Anna smiled then they walked outside of the barn to the fenced in corral. She was relieved for the fresh air and the open space. Back inside, between the two sexy men, she'd felt claustrophobic.

Both men leaned on either side of her against the fence.

She leaned against the fence and looked out between the rungs of the fence and at the horses that gathered in the corral.

"So, where did you learn how to help deliver calves?" Charlie teased.

Anna chuckled. "That was my first calf delivery."

Charlie nudged his shoulder gently into Anna's shoulder.

"It was impressive."

She smiled then she thought about her mother. Tears filled her eyes. She wrung her hands together as the scene of horses before her began to blur from her tears.

"My mom was very sick with cancer…and I took care of her," she whispered.

The men leaned in closer to her and turned to face the corral. They were taller than her, so they looked over the top rung of the fence.

"My mom used to get so clogged up with fluid or some side effect from all the medications that she was on that she would have trouble breathing. It made her panic and could set her into an anxiety attack or worse. We couldn't rush her to the hospital every time this happened, and I couldn't afford nursing care, so I took care of her on my own."

Anna sighed.

"I would talk to her calmly, try to get her to focus on my voice instead of the inability to take full breaths and, eventually, calm her down."

She wiped the tears away, embarrassed that she shared such information with Charlie and Ben. She had to admit, she trusted them and was growing fond of them.

"I don't know what the heck made me think it would work on a cow!" she blurted out then pushed away from the fence and began to walk a few steps away.

Charlie stopped her by pulling her back towards the fence between himself and Ben.

"Well, it worked, and I bet the cow is thankful, just as I'm certain your mom was thankful that you helped her through it," Charlie stated.

She felt Ben move closer behind her then move her hair off of her shoulder, away from her neck.

"It was kind of you to help out," Ben whispered then softly kissed her neck.

Anna felt the chills run over her body as she unconsciously leaned back against Ben. Charlie touched her chin.

"Yeah, thank you, Anna." Charlie kissed her.

It was short and sweet, and before she could panic, they each took her hand and began walking back toward the house.

* * * *

Anna grabbed a few things and quickly headed downstairs. After some long, hard thinking, she began to chicken out and decided sneaking into town for the night was a lot safer than being around the Cantrell men. They were lethal, and after their kisses today, she was gun-shy big time.

She was afraid of their size, their personalities, and experience. They each had a good seven, or more, years on her, and it didn't take an experienced woman to know that these men knew how to seduce a woman. She didn't want to add that to her list of "things I've done wrong in my life."

The men were rugged, attractive men, and being around them was becoming addictive. She sought them out, thought of them immediately when she landed the job today, and that wasn't normal. She shared the story about her mom with them, and that was really personal. It was scary how comfortable she felt with the men. Her trust in them could be granted prematurely. The feelings, the need to be around them was solely her hang-up and was not reciprocated by them. They merely felt sorry for her and the fucked-up life she had back in New York.

The tears stung her eyes as she thought about them. They were perfection individually, but together, they were a force. They could have their choice of a woman to share life with. They obviously had practice in their search for one.

They had to have had plenty of practice. Anna thought about that a lot. It made her jealous, and it scared her. She saw the way the women drooled over Wyatt in town. She also noticed the dirty looks she received when she entered the doctor's office. Some women had their faces practically plastered to the front window. They had to have seen Wyatt kissing her.

Then there was Ben, who always seemed to grab the attention of the ladies. That would bother her a lot. She was insecure still, and a feeling like that could cause unnecessary problems in a regular relationship, never mind one between four people. What the heck did she know? What about jealousy. When she was talking to Charlie, Ben or Wyatt would touch her. What if they got jealous of one another because of her? She could destroy their brotherly relationship.

There were so many what-ifs, but then her body and her heart reacted so strongly to each of them. Did she want them?

They each had strong characteristics of good partners. Ben was cheerful all the time, he made her laugh, and he always pulled out a chair for her or opened the door to let her in first. Charlie had a past just like hers, with his experience going through war and re-adapting to "civilization", as he called it. That conversation they had was intense and ended in one hot and heavy kiss. She warmed inside at the recollection.

Wyatt was all man. There were no hidden agendas with him. He was direct, bossy, stubborn, and...*ah, hell, I'm falling for them*!

Her number one focus should be healing up, doing well at the job tomorrow, and saving some money to leave. Now that Stacy was pregnant, it was even more important to keep her and the baby safe.

Helping with the cow today reminded her about the natural and unexpected things that could happen during a pregnancy and delivery. She wouldn't add danger into the equation. Stacy meant the world to her. She felt the ache in her belly, and fear clenched her chest. She didn't want any trouble to come to the Triple C looking for her and then have Stacy and the baby caught in the middle. The thought made her nauseous. Yet, she was scared to go off on her own. The last few weeks had been nice on the ranch. She never felt so safe, and the open air seemed to help her heal. But she couldn't be a wimp. She couldn't be so self-centered and want to be part of a family so much that she put her best friend and the baby in harm's way. That just wasn't an option.

As she slowly tiptoed out the back porch, she heard Stacy giggle and Eric and Max chuckling. She was envious as she left and hoped the three of them had a great night. How wonderful that Stacy was pregnant.

Too bad she couldn't stick around to see the baby born. But maybe in a year or two it would be safe for her to return to the Triple C and visit.

With that last thought, she slowly crept off the porch and headed around the house to the garage.

"Where do you think you're sneaking off to?"

The deep voice caused Anna to drop the bag and squeal.

Wyatt came into view as the sun began to set in the distance. She had thought that the trees provided cover, but apparently, she was wrong.

"Oh, my God, you scared me." Her heart pounded in her chest, and her legs began to shake.

"Where are you going?" he asked again, taking a few steps toward her. He looked like a man on a mission, and she felt as if he was on the hunt and she was his prey. His eyes were dark and sexy as they roamed over her body. His crew cut hair was wet. *Did he just finish taking a shower?* The thought sent a bolt of quivering desire through to her core. She focused on his clothing, relieved he wasn't wearing his uniform and was dressed casually. His jeans were loose, but snug where they should be, leaving a woman to use her imagination. His black T-shirt was stretched tight across his pectoral muscles, and his biceps looked huge. He was a big man, from her standpoint, probably the biggest of the three brothers. Anna suddenly realized his attire didn't diffuse the burning attraction inside her, it brought up the heat index. *Shit!*

"I was just going for a walk." She nibbled her bottom lip and felt her cheeks flush at the lie. Wyatt was the epitome of intimidation. The thought of him being forceful with her made her panties damp. *Damn!*

Wyatt prowled closer and now stood directly in front of her. "With an overnight bag?' he inquired, then placed his hands on his hips, tilted a little to the left as if daring her to lie some more.

Oh, boy…I'm in serious trouble.

She looked back toward the house where Stacy and her men were. No help there. The three of them were probably already in bed. Another bad direction. What was Wyatt doing to her?

She needed to focus and get him to see that her staying in town was no big deal. But first, she needed to diffuse the intense atmosphere around them.

"What about you? What are you doing?" She decided to try a different tactic. Making casual conversation might help to make her story more real.

"I was looking for you. Heard you were staying the weekend. Dinner is just about ready."

"Oh…no. I'm sorry, I'm not staying—"

Wyatt raised his eyebrows in an authoritative sort of way. She was certain when he looked at a crook that way, they confessed…on their knees. She found it sexy and way too intimidating to fight.

"Are you lying to me?" he asked softly, but with such deeper meaning and control. She felt like a child being reprimanded for getting caught with her hand in the cookie jar. Yet her body's reaction was completely different.

She shook her head.

He raised his eyebrows then gave her body the once-over again.

"You don't want to lie to me or my brothers."

His statement sent the chills through her body, but she didn't respond. It was strange, and for some odd reason, she was turned on by his statement. The feeling came out of nowhere. It was unlike anything that she ever felt before. She wanted to challenge him. She wanted to give some sort of worldly woman retort, but none came to mind. Would he punish her for lying? Put her over his knee and slap her ass?

Fudge! Where the hell did that thought come from.

Her temperature rose, and her cheeks felt inflamed.

She took a step back.

Wyatt took a step forward.

She locked gazes with him, and before she could step away again, Wyatt was pulling her into his arms.

* * * *

Wyatt couldn't take it. She looked so vulnerable and scared. He didn't want to frighten her, yet he didn't want to let her go to town. He and his brothers meant to protect her and keep her safe. With her body and sweetness, any man in town could seduce her. No fucking way were they taking a chance. This was the opportunity to get to know her and gain her trust. His brothers shared the story of her helping to deliver the calf and about her mom. He was trying his hardest to not be controlling, but it was difficult.

He held her in his arms. She was miniature compared to his own size, and the feel of her abundant breasts wedged up against his stomach increased his attraction and need to touch her. After hearing stories from Ben and Charlie about Anna and how wonderful of a person she was, Wyatt wanted to get to know her. He wanted her in every way, but still, he feared scaring her. How could he make her understand and believe that they meant her no harm but instead affection and protection?

She felt stiff and unsure in his arms. She kept her arms down by her sides as he pressed her to him. He noticed when he spoke firmly she caved in. He had the ability to get his way and to keep order and maintain the law. He never faked anything in his life. He wasn't going to start now, and especially if Anna was their one. Perhaps their little Anna needed a firm hand combined with gentle persuasion. Ben and Charlie could be the sensitive and talkative men in this relationship. If there even was a relationship growing? They were trying, but patience was never one of his strong suits.

"Put your arms around me, Anna. I need to feel them on me," he whispered, hoping his gut instinct was right.

The feel of her feminine hands slowly creeping around his waist increased the fire burning within him. He smirked but hid it from her.

He caressed her hips, then moved cautiously up her arms, over her shoulders, then took her face in his hands and tilted it up toward him. Her big, glossy, brown eyes stared up at him. He was done.

He imagined those big brown eyes looking up at him as he made love to her. Those luscious, plump lips sucking on his skin, his mouth, his cock.

He inhaled, trying to calm his breathing. This woman would break his control. There was only so long he would be able to wait to brand her his and his brothers'.

But he knew what a precious package he was dealing with, and it took pure mental control to not bend her over the car, pull her pants down, and fuck her into submission. She was not like other women. She was special.

Many different emotions and ideas went through his head. *What should I say now? What will get Anna to open up to me?*

She licked her lips, and all thoughts seized.

"I want to kiss you, Anna…can I kiss you?" he asked, as his breathing grew rapid again. This was new for him. When it came to women, he took what he wanted and what they were more than willing to give. With Anna, it was like taking baby steps, and every word, every move he made with her had to be strategic and honest. This was going to be forever. He knew it and felt it to his core.

She was silent as he began to lower himself to reach her lips.

"Please tell me yes, darling, then we'll go inside and have some supper."

Her eyes sparkled, and he felt her raspy breath but got no answer from her. Her silence was a yes, and right before he took her lips, she closed her eyes in anticipation and silent agreement to his request.

Thank the Lord.

Her mouth was warm and silky. Her taste and her own desire filled him as he devoured every inch of her mouth. What started out as slow and gentle soon turned into erotic and hot. He couldn't get enough, and the feel of Anna's hands touching him, caressing him, and battling for control of the kiss caused his cock to throb against the zipper of his pants.

Wyatt reached down to the hem of her shirt, wanting to feel more of her skin against his own. The moment he touched the bandage, he paused unconsciously, angry at the fact she had such intense injuries. Anna took that moment to pull away.

They were breathless but held one another's gaze.

She covered her mouth with her hands. He saw the tears fill her eyes then her turn away from him. Her shoulders shook, and she held herself. He damned his reaction to the bandages.

"Anna. I'm sorry." He reached for her, but she held her position. Her head was down, and then he heard her sobs.

* * * *

It had been a perfect kiss. One that made her insides coil, her toes curl within her sneakers, and her panties wet. It was ruined the moment Wyatt touched her bandages and tensed. He didn't want to touch her. He didn't really care. Her father, her past ruined everything, even this special moment between her and Wyatt.

She couldn't control the deep sobs that racked her body. Then, suddenly, she heard him whisper, plead for her to look at him, but she feared what she would see. She gave so much in that kiss. She took a chance and allowed the sensations to run and be free. What did he really want with her?

Anna felt his arms around her, then the sensation of being lifted off the ground. She was in his arms an instant later.

"Anna, baby, look at me, please," he asked, and when she gazed up, she was shocked at the sadness reflected in Wyatt's eyes. *I must be losing my mind*. She figured as much as the embarrassment kicked in, and his strong arms felt too good to not continue to desire.

The smell of his cologne, the slight hint of cigar tobacco filled her senses. He was manly and sexy, and she needed him this close. Anna held on as Wyatt squatted to reach her bag then stood in a quick motion with little effort, despite the fact that he held her in his arms.

They walked across the yard. The sun was no longer in sight, just the imprints in the sky of its path upon setting.

"What's wrong? Is she okay?"

She heard Charlie's voice, then Ben's, as Wyatt reached the doorway.

They must have exchanged some silent understanding or comments that she didn't hear because they simply stepped out of the way as Wyatt entered the doorway with her in his arms.

She kept her face against his chest, not wanting the others to see her so helpless and so upset. "*Just bring me to my room and leave me here, please,*" she thought to herself as Wyatt placed her down on a bed.

The room was huge, and the bed just as big and covered with fluffy pillows. The suede comforter was gorgeous and masculine, just like Wyatt.

He sat next to her with one arm over her waist. Then he reached for her, she closed her eyes and felt him gently caress the tears away.

When she opened them, three sets of dark brown eyes looked back at her. They were filled with concern. The air was so thick it was practically suffocating her.

"Is this the guest room?" she asked, damning her voice for cracking.

"No. This is my room," Wyatt stated.

She swallowed hard and tried to sit up.

"I thought you said that you had a guest room for me to use?"

"After you just tried to sneak off to town alone, I'm not taking any chances," he replied.

"What?"

"She did what?" Ben, then Charlie, asked.

Their facial expressions warned her that they were upset, but she held her ground.

She sat up and planted her feet on the floor.

All three men loomed over her.

* * * *

Charlie was pissed, and as he absorbed the information that Anna tried to sneak off to town, he nearly lost it. There were men that were interested in Anna despite Wyatt's public proclamation. He and his brothers weren't taking the chance of losing her.

As she sat up, he absorbed the sight of her. Her hair was ruffled from lying down on Wyatt's bed, and her blouse loosened, revealing some sort of lacy camisole beneath. It showed a lot more cleavage then he was certain Anna intended. He would make certain that she knew she couldn't walk around flaunting her assets like that. At least not around anyone but them.

The thought of another man touching her or trying to make a move caused a crazy reaction inside of him.

He grabbed Anna by her hand and pulled her up to him. She squealed right before he covered her mouth in a deep kiss.

Charlie held both her hands behind her back then used his other hand to hold her head in place as he kissed her.

The feel of her tiny, delicate wrists fitting in one of his hands had his cock throbbing with the need to possess Anna.

He was relieved when she didn't pull away, but instead, she moaned against his mouth.

The kiss lasted a long time, and when he finally released her lips, they were swollen and red.

"In every good, strong relationship, there has to be honesty. So we're gonna be honest with you, Anna. My brothers and I want you," Charlie announced as Ben moved in behind Anna, prepared to stop her if she tried to bolt. He was pleasantly surprised when she didn't move. She stood in front of him with her lips full and her cheeks flushed.

"We are going to protect you, possess you body and soul and love, and provide for you, so there's no use in fighting it."

He pulled her back against his chest and began kissing her again before she could protest.

He nearly yelled a halleluiah when he felt her hands rub against his chest. Anna began kissing him back with just as much passion as his own.

* * * *

Anna didn't know what came over her. One minute, she wanted to run for her life, and the next, she wanted to throw inhibition to the wind with a loud, "Fuck it!"

She blamed it on her age, her inexperience, the fresh air, anything else other than pure lust for the three brothers. They were hot. They wanted her, and damn it, she wanted them. She wanted all of what they offered.

Then her mind, and perhaps her fear of trusting again, took over. She clenched her eyes tighter in an attempt to will the images away.

The feel of muscle beneath her fingertips scared her, and as Ben closed in behind her, the flashbacks began. She opened her eyes. She knew it was Charlie and Ben, but then her heart began to race with uncertainty. She closed her eyes and tried to focus on the feel of their hands and the fact that it was Ben and Charlie touching her, but the images wouldn't stop.

The men from New York penetrated her mind. She fought for control but lost the battle as she swore she smelled the cologne that the other men wore.

She felt herself begin to shake, and the tears started.

Charlie paused, then she felt Ben stop, but she wouldn't open her eyes. How could she face them and admit she was so scared and weak. They would surely think she was an immature child instead of the type of woman they needed and were used to. She was certain as she clenched her eyes and tried to stop the shaking.

* * * *

"Anna, baby, what's wrong?" Wyatt heard Charlie ask, but his attention was on Anna. She was shaking, the tears were flowing, and instantly, he knew they had pushed her too far too soon. Or maybe she was in pain.

"You shouldn't have pulled her so hard," Ben stated from behind Anna.

"I didn't pull her hard. Anna, did I hurt you?" Charlie whispered as he caressed the tears away from her cheek.

"Move away from her now," Wyatt stated, loud enough that he noticed Anna jump at his voice, then hug herself.

He slowly walked toward her but not before locking gazes with his brothers. Both looked shocked and worried that they had actually done something to hurt Anna.

Wyatt gently pulled Anna into an embrace.

"What is it, Anna? Did they hurt you?" he asked.

"Hurt her! We didn't hurt her!" Ben exclaimed, and both he and Charlie began arguing.

"Stop it!" Anna exclaimed, instantly causing the men to shut their mouths and look at her and Wyatt.

Anna looked shy and embarrassed as she tilted her head up toward Wyatt and nibbled her bottom lip. Damn, he loved when she did that, even though it usually meant she felt nervous.

"They…they didn't hurt me, Wyatt," she whispered, and the silky sound of her voice had his cock throbbing against his fly. He had to maintain his composure. He wouldn't hurt Anna. He wouldn't push her to be intimate if she wasn't ready yet.

"Then what is it, doll? Talk to us so we can help you," he replied as he placed one hand on her waist while he wiped the tears away from her cheeks with his other hand.

He smiled softly, and she blushed before she looked down toward the floor. Yeah…she wanted them as much as they wanted her, but something stood in the way. Was it the ménage relationship and being with three men? It would kill him inside if she couldn't handle it and wasn't interested. Or, perhaps it was the idea of having sex with three men when she was used to one. Bad thought! The idea of her with another man got his blood boiling. He tightened his jaw, and Anna flinched. He hadn't even seen her staring at him.

"Don't be angry with me. It wasn't them or you. It's me," she blurted out as the tears began to fall again.

"I'm not angry with you, darling. I want to know how I can take that scared look off your face and make you smile. I love to see you smile," he stated.

"What did we do, Anna? Whatever scared you, please tell us so we don't do it again," Ben added from the side of them.

Wyatt watched as Anna looked toward Ben and Charlie.

"You didn't do anything wrong. It's just that…I felt…I felt trapped."

"Trapped!" both Charlie and Ben asked, and Wyatt felt his own gut clench. This wasn't going to work. *Fuck!*

Chapter 9

"Please, don't be angry with me. I was…I was enjoying the kisses and the feel of your hands on me…" Anna blushed.

Wyatt tilted her chin up toward him.

"What then?"

"It's not fair. It's just not fair that I can't get the thoughts out of my head."

"What thoughts?" Wyatt asked as he glanced toward Ben and Charlie.

"The night the men broke into the apartment. The way they touched me, and what they wanted to do to me—"

"We made you feel that way?" Charlie asked in a loud voice. It was obvious he was insulted and upset at her statement.

"No…no, Charlie," Anna immediately exclaimed, placing a hand on his arm.

Wyatt still held her close, and now Ben moved in behind her again. She felt him place a hand on her shoulder, and the tears filled her eyes.

He pulled away.

Wyatt saw his response to her tears. His brothers were afraid that she was scared of them even though she just said she wasn't.

"It's me, not you, guys," Anna added, straining her neck to look at each of them. They surrounded her again. It was no use. They couldn't stop getting close to her.

"Explain, Anna, so we can help you," Wyatt offered.

"I know you wouldn't hurt me. I want to believe everything you're telling me. I want to give this relationship a try, really, I do."

"But?" Charlie asked, taking her hand into his own.

"I couldn't help it. You're all so big and so intimidating. You're probably used to more mature and experienced women, and I'm not used to getting any attention, never mind three gorgeous, sexy men. I don't know why the thoughts entered my head, you're not like those men, and I know it was a scary experience, so I probably just need time to get over it. I'm weak…that's what it is," Anna rambled on and on, then began to cry again.

"You think we're gorgeous and sexy?" Ben whispered against her ear.

She snorted and giggled. Leave it to Ben to think that was the most important information in Anna's statement.

Wyatt knew she was scared and uncertain. He could deal with that, but what he couldn't deal with was if she wasn't attracted to them.

"Ahh, baby, you're not weak. On the contrary to all the crazy feelings you have inside, you're quite special and stronger than any woman we've ever known," Wyatt told her, then pulled her close and kissed her forehead.

"You're also the sexiest woman we ever laid eyes on. Now, I don't know what type of men you've been with, honey, but apparently, they didn't know shit about how to treat a woman. Your pleasure and your happiness is our number one priority," Charlie added, then lifted her hand to his lips before kissing it.

She jumped a little as she felt the second set of hands on her shoulders as Ben began to touch her.

"Don't let those thoughts scare you, Anna. Just lean on us, and we'll take care of you," Ben whispered next to her ear.

* * * *

She closed her eyes and absorbed the feel of all three men touching her. They thought she had experience with men. Jesus! She was in serious trouble. She couldn't lie to them or pull off experienced even if she wanted to. She'd never seen a man naked, never mind three at once. She might have a damn heart attack. How embarrassing would that be? No, she wouldn't think about her inadequacies. She needed to finally trust someone other than herself and Stacy. She needed to trust a man if she were ever going to fall in love and have a normal relationship. The thought of loving them should not have entered her mind. Her belly ached as she swallowed hard.

Charlie, Ben, and Wyatt wouldn't hurt her, at least not intentionally.

Anna felt Ben's lips against her neck, and she closed her eyes, was lost in sensation after sensation. Ben caressed her shoulders first, then her back to her hips and across her backside. He whispered in her ear as Charlie tilted her chin up toward him and covered her mouth in a sensual kiss. She felt him sweep his tongue around her mouth then nibble on her lower lip.

Wyatt slowly moved his hands over her hips and under her blouse. He caressed the bandages against her ribs, and she didn't feel pain, just warmth and tingling. As the three of them caressed her, licked and kissed her skin, she began to relax and slowly allow her body to react to them. She swayed back toward Ben, then forward toward Charlie. She sought out Wyatt, needed him there, too.

Wyatt's hands were extra large, his fingertips, long and thick, moved over her skin and across her bra. He cupped her breasts, and she moaned at the sensation as he attempted to gather every inch of them into his palms.

Charlie released her lips then pulled her blouse and camisole over her head and off of her.

She tried to cover herself, but Wyatt's hands still massaged her breasts, and one look at Charlie had her heart pounding inside her chest.

"You're gorgeous, Anna. Never cover yourself up in front of us," Charlie told her, then touched his fingers to her lips before giving her a quick kiss ending with a slight lick of his tongue to her skin.

She blushed, then inhaled, raising her breasts to Wyatt's touch. Simultaneously, Ben raised her arms up and against his neck. She felt his hardness against her ass, and she closed her eyes, feeling her body crave more of their touch.

"We are going to take care of you, Anna. It's going to be our pleasure to kiss, suck, and possess every inch of your fucking perfect body," Charlie whispered low against her neck.

She felt the chills cover her body at his explicit language. This was all so new to her, yet her pussy clenched at his words and their touch. She felt the wetness and moaned as Wyatt pinched her nipple. Ben undid the clasp to her bra then removed the lacy material. All three men inhaled and stared at her.

Before she could feel completely embarrassed, Wyatt squatted then leaned forward, taking her nipple and part of the breast into his mouth. She grabbed his head as Ben released her arms. Charlie caressed her other breast then leaned down to take a taste for himself.

Anna moaned as she held their heads against her. It felt so good. God, she never imagined it would feel like this.

As they kissed and sucked, she felt Charlie and Wyatt move their hands up her thighs.

She tilted her mound toward their hands, and they mumbled against her breast, which caused tiny vibrations to invade her body.

She wanted more, and they read her body, rubbing their hands over her mound and against the material covering it.

"I love this ass. It's firm and round, made for a man to hold on to while he's fucking his woman from behind."

Anna moaned at Ben's words. No one ever spoke to her like that. She never had one lover, never mind three. Her pussy clenched, and she felt the moisture against her panties. She cried out, amazed that their touch and words alone made her come.

"Fuck, baby! That was fucking incredible," Ben stated against her ear before nibbling on her lobe.

Wyatt and Charlie began removing her bottoms.

"Do you feel how hard my cock is?" Ben whispered. His erotic words were doing a number on her body. She felt herself tighten again and about ready to burst.

She was naked in front of them now, with only her black thong bikini underwear.

Ben's fingers caressed her from front to back. When he lifted the string between her ass cheeks, she tightened. He bent down, kissed and licked her lower spine, then each cheek.

Charlie and Wyatt devoured her breasts still, and she felt the fingers caress her pussy lips. Charlie's hands rubbed and fondled her then Wyatt pushed a finger inside her. She threw her head back and moaned at the invasion.

"Oh, God, Wyatt!" She grabbed his hand. At first, she shook with fear and anticipation, but then, the rhythm of the in and out motion, combined with the sensations running through her body, made her hips move with him.

"She's got the best fucking ass. I can't wait to fuck this ass. You like that idea, Anna?"

Before she could answer, Charlie was touching her chin and tilting her face up toward him. She swallowed hard at the look in his eyes. It was carnal and intense.

He took her mouth with his teeth. He gently pulled the bottom lip first before fully kissing her, plunging in deep with his tongue and tasting every inch of her. Wyatt continued to finger her, adding another digit, then bending lower, placing his mouth on her pussy lips. The sensation of his fingers and his tongue nibbling on her clit sent her into another orgasm. She spread her legs, and he lifted one over his shoulder, baring her completely to his mouth and eyes.

She grabbed Charlie's shoulder, and Ben took that moment to rub a finger over the moisture and caress her lips then trace back over the puckered hole. She gasped at the idea of them taking her there.

"I want to fuck this tight, beautiful ass, Anna. Has anyone ever fucked your ass?" He growled against her skin, lightly biting her cheeks then licking the slit.

"Oh, God, no!" she screamed.

The sounds of Wyatt sucking her cream away filled the bedroom.

"I think she likes that idea, Ben. What do you think, Wyatt?" Charlie asked as he lowered himself next to Wyatt.

"Fucking delicious. She tastes so good." Wyatt flicked his tongue and pumped his fingers deeper into Anna's channel.

She heard a zipper go down, and her heart raced. He wasn't going to take her there, was he?

"No! Stop!" she blurted out, pulling away from the three of them.

They all looked crazed with desire, and she immediately felt the loss of their touch and embrace, but she had to be honest. She couldn't let them think she was more experienced than she let on so far.

"What is it?" Ben asked.

She stared at him. At some point, he'd removed his shirt, and his impeccable abs were a sight for the eyes. He was firm, trim, and oh, God, his crotch. A small patch of light brown hair below his navel stretched clear into his package. The mushroom top was sticking out, and by the look of the bulge, he was generous in the penis department.

"I…I'm."

Ben looked at her as if he understood her fear, and that confident, cocky stud had the nerve to whip out his cock and point it toward her.

She was fascinated by its appearance and size. It was quite a beautiful sight. Thick, lighter than the rest of his tanned complexion, and she licked her lips.

"Oh, baby, you're killing me," Ben whispered in a raspy voice.

Wyatt took her hand and led her to the bed.

"Talk to us," he stated, and she got the chills from his demanding tone.

"I've never done this," she whispered, still staring at Ben's cock and his mischievous smile.

"A virgin ass? Fucking love it!" Ben exclaimed, and Anna lowered her eyes.

Charlie tilted her head up toward them.

She saw the concern in his face as well as a small dimple in his left cheek. She loved his dimples. He was so handsome, with light brown hair and big brown eyes. She felt the calluses on his fingertips and his rough demeanor. He was mysterious in a lot of ways.

"Don't be afraid. If you're not ready for that, we'll take things slow. But one day real soon, we're all going to take you at once," Charlie stated with confidence.

Anna licked her lips and leaned back with her elbows and forearms against the bed. Wyatt lay on his side beside her now, and Ben still stood in front of her, holding his cock, smirking.

She giggled at his personality. He was such a tease.

In nervousness, she licked her lips again, and the three men moaned.

"You keep licking those lips, and I'll give you something to suck on, Anna," Charlie exclaimed, pulling his shirt up over his head, then, he began to unzip his pants.

Anna knew she had to tell them.

"I've never done that before, either."

All three of them looked at each other, then back at Anna.

This time, Wyatt responded.

"Never what, Anna?" Wyatt asked softly.

"Suck cock?" Ben interjected, and both Wyatt and Charlie gave him a dirty look.

Anna felt herself redden.

She nodded.

"Wow…well, don't worry. We'll take it slow, baby," Charlie whispered, then removed his jeans the rest of the way and lay down beside her on the other side.

"No! You don't understand. God, this is so embarrassing." Anna covered her face with her hands.

A few seconds passed before she felt hands caressing her from head to toe. Then Wyatt removed her hands from her face.

"Hey, now, there's no need to be embarrassed because you're not as experienced."

"Yeah, I kind of like the fact that that mouth won't suck any other cocks than ours," Ben stated.

"Ben!" Wyatt, Charlie, and Anna exclaimed.

"What?" he asked, shrugging his shoulders, but still held his long, thick cock in his fist.

"Umm…we said we were going to be completely honest, right?" Anna asked as she looked at each of them. Her mouth watered at the sight. They were sexy as damn hell, and she still couldn't believe that they wanted her.

"Of course, Anna."

She smiled at Charlie.

"Well, about this whole experience thing," she whispered, then clasped her fingers together.

"Yes," all three men chimed in.

"I'm a virgin!" she blurted out, then covered her face again.

"What?" they yelled, and she cringed.

A few seconds of silence passed between them, and she slowly uncovered her eyes.

All three men stared at her. Their eyes were dark and mesmerizing. Their breathing grew rapid as they adjusted their positions. She felt like a trapped animal about to be devoured by its predators.

"Never, Anna?" Ben asked in a whisper.

She shook her head, and a moment later, they were all over her like white on rice.

Chapter 10

"Oh, God!" Anna exclaimed.

Ben spread her thighs and immediately plunged his tongue into her pussy. There was no hesitation, just a lustful need to ravage her there. She reached down to hold him.

She screamed at the invasion and lifted her hips toward his mouth. God, it felt so damn good. The pain in her ribs didn't halt her movements.

"You were meant to be ours, baby. You'll always be just ours," Charlie exclaimed as he cupped her breasts, then leaned forward to take her nipple into his mouth.

She locked gazes with Wyatt.

Oh, God, he looked pissed, or maybe just carnal and needy.

"Ours. All fucking ours." His voice sounded like a growl, then he covered her mouth with his own. Wyatt kissed her for a long time. His tongue explored deeply, nearly knocking the wind out of her. He was caressing the inside of her mouth, and she tasted him as well. He was so masculine and hot. The taste of cigar and mint penetrated her taste buds. He was much older and sophisticated. Everything about him was a turn-on. From his crew cut hair and massive build to his uniform and authoritative attitude. He was the law, and what he said went. She stirred inside.

* * * *

Wyatt knew it was chauvinistic and selfish, but the fact that Anna was a virgin in every sense of the word made him want to possess her and own her. By Ben and Charlie's response to her admittance, they felt just as compelled to be her firsts.

When he felt the bandages against her ribs and felt the anxiety as she admitted her fears to them, he paused to think things through. There really was no reason to rush and claim her. She was attracted to them, and she was here with them now. Was there really a need to rush?

Wyatt held her gaze, and before he could question whether she wanted to continue, her hands were grabbing him, pulling him closer for a kiss.

She kissed with passion, her mouth delicate beneath his, and his heart soared.

"My turn," Wyatt heard Charlie state as he took Ben's place between Anna's legs. Now, Ben joined them on the bed.

"Your cream is so fucking delicious." He kissed her and plunged his tongue into her mouth.

* * * *

Anna moaned. She was shocked at Ben's words but thrilled that he liked licking her down there. She never would have imagined being feasted on like this. All the sensations, all their techniques and moves, had her head spinning out of control. She reached for his head and met his kisses tongue at tongue. What a way to fight. Surely, there were no losers in this type of battle.

She absorbed every sensation and taste. When she tasted herself on Ben's tongue and in his mouth, she felt so naughty and excited. Anna had forbidden herself to ever feel any attraction for a man like this. This type of exposure of flesh, carnal and explicit actions, weren't ever even thoughts or fantasies in her mind. But with these three men, she wanted, just wanted, and wanted so very much.

When Ben finally released her lips, nibbling her bottom lip between his teeth, he held her gaze as if he, too, felt the power of their kiss.

"Your breasts are perfect. Plump, round, and I love these pretty pink nipples," Ben whispered, blowing air across the tips.

"Aren't they perfect?" Wyatt added from the other side of her, squeezing her other breast before he leaned closer to kiss her lips.

Anna moaned against Wyatt's mouth as Charlie pushed two fingers inside her and nibbled her clit. It was like nothing she ever felt before. Three simultaneous and different touches to her flesh. She wiggled and moaned against Wyatt's mouth. Surely, one could die from such sensations.

Charlie pressed fingers in and out of her channel. It was deep and sent a quiver of moisture and desire through her core. She lifted her hips, and by no account of her own conscious mind, she began to lift and push against his digit. She held a hand against Ben and Wyatt's head as they feasted on her breasts. Damn, she wanted more. Where was this need coming from?

She arched her hips and cringed for a moment at the pinch of pain in her ribs.

All three of them stopped.

* * * *

Anna was panting, and the moment the sensations stopped and Charlie released his hold, simultaneously with Ben and Wyatt, her heart ached.

"What? What's wrong?" she asked, frightened that she did something to turn them off and upset them. Damn it, she didn't know what she was doing. Were they turned off because she humped his fingers, wanting more? How embarrassing. She never felt like this before, and she didn't want them to stop. She nearly demanded them to continue, but as she reached for Charlie's hand, he held it firmly against her calf.

Charlie gently touched her bandages with his other hand.

"Are you in pain?" he asked, and she quickly glanced at all three of them, wanting to demand they stop pampering her and fuck her already. She wanted to feel them inside her, and she couldn't stand the wait. But instead, she softened her outrage when she saw the concern on their faces.

They cared so much about her that they were willing to stop their own sexual need to keep her safe? Unbelievable. The thought that they cared so much about her brought tears to her eyes.

"Anna?" Ben whispered.

"I'm not in pain." She sniffled and wiped the tears from her eyes.

"Then why are you crying?" Charlie asked.

She didn't want to ruin the moment and act like a blubbering idiot. Damn, her twenty-three years would surely show against these older men. She took a deep breath, and still they waited, touching her with soothing, gentle caresses.

"Because you stopped," she stated.

"We stopped because you flinched as if you were in pain," Ben replied, on the defensive.

Anna smiled at them.

"I want you to continue. I need you to make love to me and show me that you care and that you're going to protect me. I want you to take my virginity and do it now!" She yelled then felt the heat reach her cheeks at her outburst. She nibbled her bottom lips.

Charlie smiled then removed his boxers. He reached down, picked up a condom out of his pants pocket, and put it in place.

"In that case, darling, let us begin showering you with our love and affection."

Her insides fluttered, and her stomach clenched as Charlie caressed her thighs, pushing them farther apart.

Wyatt and Ben were on either side of her helping to relax her and make her feel safe.

The feel of three sets of hands covering and caressing her body brought on waves of excitement but also a feeling of belonging.

One look at Charlie's cock and Anna smiled before he slowly pushed inside her.

It was a slow, torturous push that had her panting for air the further he went. He was big, and she wondered if it would fit. Damn, it felt so hard and so good. Charlie clenched his teeth and growled but was determined.

Anna tried to relax, but there was so much anticipation, and she had waited a long time to give her virginity away. She wanted this and craved the feel of each of the men inside her.

She looked at Charlie. First, his thighs as he bent showing off his muscles, then she absorbed his gorgeous pectoral muscles and chest. There were multiple dark lines hidden beneath his chest hair. But before she could figure out what they were, her eyes roamed over the rest of him. He had a dusting of hair across it that met in one thin line toward his cock. She licked her lips then lost focus a moment when she felt Ben and Wyatt.

Ben nibbled on one nipple as Wyatt pinched and rolled her other nipple, enhancing the sensation of Charlie pushing further into her channel.

She felt her vaginal walls clamp down and tighten as Charlie fought for control then growled again before he shoved forward, instantly penetrating the small barrier and burying his cock to the hilt.

"Arrrr!" He roared with relief, and Anna moaned, tossing her head to the side.

She felt so full. There was an onslaught of sensations as Charlie pressed in and out of her channel, initially slow, then harder and faster with each thrust.

"That's it, baby. Damn, Anna, you're so tight and hot. I feel you holding me in place, and I can't take it. It's so fucking good," he growled.

Wyatt massaged her breast then covered her mouth, kissing her.

Ben licked and pulled on her nipple then spread kisses along her chest. Their hands caressed her inner thighs, pulling them higher and wider so Charlie could get deeper inside her, and it was all too much to handle as an orgasm overtook her body. She screamed her release against Wyatt's mouth as Charlie thrust hard, exploding inside of her.

Wyatt released her lips, smiled, then slid off the bed.

Charlie lay over her, being sure not to crush her ribs or apply too much pressure, but he wanted to kiss her.

"That was fantastic."

She smiled at him and cupped his face between her feminine hands before kissing his lips.

She absorbed the sight of his muscular chest and multitude of scars. She knew her face showed concern, but she couldn't help but wonder what happened to him.

"It's all right, Anna. Just a few war wounds."

He pulled from her body and rolled to the side, taking Wyatt's place.

When she looked to the side, Ben was there, and he leaned over to kiss her long and hard.

She was lost in his kiss when she felt a set of hands on her thighs and another cock at her entrance.

"My turn, sweetheart," Wyatt whispered as Ben released her lips, and her gaze locked with Wyatt's.

He placed his hands against her thighs, rubbed them gently, causing her to giggle. He gave her one of his cocky, sexy grins and slowly began to push forward.

Anna and Wyatt held each other's gazes during the slow process.

She felt a deep connection as each of them took her. It was instant and powerful as she relished in the feeling of being part of them.

He clenched his teeth and titled his hips forward, and Anna counter-pushed to get him inside her faster. The move set Wyatt off, his resistance diminished by Anna's response.

* * * *

He was huge and solid, but her body wanted every inch of the three of them.

She knew Wyatt was a full throttle kind of man as he took what he wanted yet still remained aware of her injuries.

His thrusts were long and torturous as he lifted her hips to see how far he could push her before she would feel pain from her ribs.

The sensation of being filled with his cock was too good to resist, so she clenched her teeth and pushed along with him.

They rocked the bed and left little room for Ben and Charlie to join them, but somehow, they did.

"I love watching my brother fuck you, honey, but I need you, too," Ben whispered, and when she was able to focus on him, she saw him sitting up with his cock fisted in his hand.

Anna licked her lips, and Wyatt growled then thrust harder and faster.

"I need to feel that mouth on me. Can you try it, honey?"

She stretched her neck closer and smiled right before she took her first taste of heaven.

Ben moaned then held her hair and head as he pumped inside Anna's mouth.

"Fuck, that's hot!" Wyatt yelled, then pumped in rhythm with Ben's thrusts.

Anna felt hunger like she never had before as she sucked, licked, and nibbled on Ben. At first, she felt like gagging, but Charlie was beside her whispering words of encouragement and technique. She loved that they accepted her inexperience, even relished in the thought of them being her firsts. After today, there was no going back to her old self. She wanted more of them. As much as she could get.

Wyatt grabbed her ass as he fucked her harder and harder. She felt him reach down and rub her, and her body hummed. Before she knew what he was doing, she felt his finger rub over her puckered hole, then push inside.

She screamed her release against Ben's cock, sucking, licking, and pulling harder than at first.

Ben kept a speedy pace, and the more she sucked and hummed, the harder he got. He fisted her hair in his hand, and the slight pain turned her on. She wasn't frightened, instead, she felt wanton and exotic.

"That's it, baby, just like that. Damn that mouth, I can't hold out, I'm coming, honey."

"Me, too!" Wyatt exclaimed as he pumped faster. The bed frame banged against the wall as Charlie latched on to her breast and nipped her hard. Ben tried to pull out of Anna's mouth, but Anna held him in place, caressed his balls with her fingertips, and swallowed as fast as she could while he exploded down her throat. She just kept licking and licking, loving the taste and feel of Ben's essence.

He was pleading for mercy, and she wondered what was wrong with him.

Charlie and Wyatt chuckled as Ben clenched his teeth in agony. Finally, she released him.

"Did I hurt you? Did I do something wrong?" she asked, confused and out of breath.

Ben leaned forward and covered her mouth with his own, kissing her wildly before finally releasing her lips.

"Not one fucking thing wrong, Anna. You're a natural."

That brought a smile to her face as Wyatt thrust his cock one last time before pulling from her body. Charlie pulled her into his arms and kissed her.

Chapter 11

Anna felt the fingers against her neck, and she couldn't breathe. The hot breath against her shoulder and ear made her want to hurl. She tried to fight her attacker, but his hold was strong, and he lifted her off the ground like a rag doll. She screamed for him to let go and to leave her alone, but he laughed. She kicked him, her foot landing against his inner thigh, causing him to loosen his hold. She fell to the ground, her ribs throbbed, but she clawed at the dirt to escape. He was on her in an instant, ripping her dress off of her, revealing her body to his evil eyes.

She spit at him, her only weapon of defense before he slapped her across the mouth. He beat on her and spread her legs. "You filthy whore! I killed your men, now, you're mine!"

Anna screamed, kicked, and cried for help until suddenly she heard Wyatt's voice. He was yelling at her.

* * * *

"Wake up, damn it!" Wyatt demanded. Wyatt and Ben tried to get Anna to come out of the nightmare.

Finally, what seemed like many minutes had passed, she jerked upright, the tears streaming down her cheeks.

Wyatt and Ben both spoke to her.

"Honey, you're all right. You're with us," Wyatt stated.

"God, baby! That was scary," Ben added as he caressed her arms.

Anna looked at both of them before closing her eyes.

Wyatt lay on his elbow next to her as she clung on to the sheet.

"I'm sorry," she whispered, then rolled into Wyatt, clinging to his chest.

He wrapped his arms around her, holding her tight against him.

"Does that happen every night?" Ben asked while he caressed her shoulders and back, placing tiny kisses along her shoulders.

She nodded her head.

Wyatt clenched his teeth and locked gazes with his brother.

They shared the same anger and look of concern.

Anna tilted her head up toward Wyatt. "Where's Charlie?"

"He had to go out and check on a few of the animals. One of the mares was sick the last few days," Wyatt whispered, then placed his hand against her cheek.

He stared at the leftover tears clinging to her long, dark eyelashes. His chest tightened.

"Baby, I thought Doc Jones gave you something to help you sleep," he inquired.

"I don't like the way they make me feel. I'm all drowsy in the morning and unaware of where I am when I first wake up."

He gave her a look as if scolding her for not following doctor's orders.

"Tonight, you are taking them. We're here for you," Ben added over her shoulder as he pressed his erection between her ass cheeks.

She closed her eyes and felt herself blush at the sensation.

Wyatt kissed her lips, rolled to his back, taking her with him.

Anna straddled his hips and was grateful that her hips weren't the least bit sore.

They fought one another for control over the kiss, and Anna rubbed her mound against his hard cock. She felt the bed dip then give as Ben left the bed but returned a few seconds later.

Wyatt released her lips and scooted toward the edge of the bed so his legs hung off.

"I want to feel that hot, tight pussy, baby. Come on, now," he growled at her, then effortlessly lifted her up, placing her onto his engorged cock.

Anna threw her head back and moaned at the intrusion. She was sore from last night but wet and ready for her sheriff.

The thought made her smile.

"I love the way your tits swing and bounce when we're making love. It was all I dreamt about last night," Wyatt whispered as he fondled and played with her breasts while she rode him. Anna picked up the pace until she felt Ben move in behind her.

"You trust us, baby, don't ya?" Ben asked as he slowly pressed her down further against Wyatt's chest.

She nodded, and Wyatt took her mouth again while he plunged up and down into her.

Anna joined the rhythm, lifting and thrusting onto his cock and loving the feeling of control.

She felt Ben's hands caress her ass cheeks, and she paused a moment to catch her breath.

"Easy, darling. We're going to take this nice and slow."

"What, Ben?" she asked, out of breath with anticipation.

"I want to fuck this tight, pretty, virgin ass of yours, darling. I'm just gonna get you ready," he whispered as he kissed her neck, sucking hard as he rubbed his engorged cock against her ass.

Wyatt reached between them and played with her lips before spreading some cream along her puckered hole.

Anna gasped at the sensation, while Ben lightly held her chest down against Wyatt's.

Wyatt pressed his finger in, while he pumped up and into her channel.

"Ahhhh...Oh my." Anna moaned while she held on to Wyatt.

Then she felt something cold and moist as Ben pressed his finger into her anus. She moaned, then wiggled her ass, wanting his fingers deeper to increase the pleasure pain she felt.

It was erotic and burned her insides, yet her pussy flooded with moisture in response.

"That's it, Anna, just like that, fuck my fingers while you fuck Wyatt's cock," Ben whispered as he pressed his body against Anna's and thrust his finger onto her. She moved up and down, back and forth whatever way possible so she could feel more of the strange sensation.

Ben added a second finger and thrust in and out while scissoring side to side.

Anna moaned then pressed forward as Wyatt pulled her mouth to his.

He kissed her deeply while he ground his hips up and into her. He scooted lower on the bed as Ben pulled his fingers out. Anna protested until she felt his cock take their place.

"Relax, honey, and we'll make you feel so good." Ben pressed forward, and Wyatt nibbled lightly on Anna's tongue.

Anna lifted up, then back, forcing Ben to shove into her faster than he intended.

"Fuck, Anna!" he growled as he grabbed her hips to stop her movements.

"I could have hurt you!" he scolded.

Anna moaned, too absorbed with the feeling of fullness.

The fact that she ignored his reprimand seemed to egg him on as Ben let loose with everything he had.

In and out, up and down, her men pounded into her. One second, one was buried balls deep then, the next second, another was. It was too much, and she couldn't control her body, the awkward movements. She just held on and embraced the feelings of being possessed by them.

"She's so fucking tight!" Ben yelled as he bit down lightly on her shoulder.

Ben held her shoulders, pushing down, simultaneously sending Wyatt deeper inside her. Wyatt increased his pace, and she felt both hard cocks and knew they were going to come. Her whole body tightened and spiraled out of control, just a little more, that's all she needed.

Wyatt took that second to pull her nipple while biting and sucking her neck. She exploded, and so did her men.

The aftershocks lasted a few more minutes as the three of them held on to each other, embracing the closeness of what they just shared.

Ben slowly pulled out first and walked to the bathroom. Wyatt pulled out next and rolled Anna to her side, holding her against his chest.

She closed her eyes and caught her breath.

"Amazing!" she stated as Ben returned, and Wyatt chuckled.

He tweaked her nipple, and she stirred next to him.

"Hey."

"Hey, yourself," he whispered next to her then kissed her lips.

Ben crawled onto the bed with a warm, soapy washcloth to clean her.

He leaned across her body, touched her breasts then kissed her.

"You are incredible, Anna, and I love this body," he whispered as he finished taking care of her and caressed her breasts after being thorough down below.

Anna smiled and cuddled closer to Wyatt as Ben snuggled against the back of her.

* * * *

After showers and breakfast, everyone met downstairs. Wyatt was dressed in his uniform, ready to give her a ride to the restaurant. Charlie stopped by before she left.

He took her into his arms, kissed her then gave her a playful slap across her butt.

"Hey!" she exclaimed as she pulled away, smiling.

He shook a finger at her. "You watch how friendly you get with the guys in town, or I'll be spanking that ass until it's pink."

Anna laughed at him. He couldn't be serious. She looked at Wyatt, then at Ben, for confirmation that Charlie was teasing, but the seriousness in their eyes told her otherwise. She swallowed hard. The thought of them spanking her should have been frightening. Instead, she felt the dampness between her legs, and the temperature seemed to heighten. *Yikes!*

"You better stop giving those looks, darling, or you'll miss your first day at work," Ben teased then kissed her just as thoroughly as Charlie.

Anna smiled then waved good-bye as she got into Wyatt's truck.

Chapter 12

Anna guzzled down the cold glass of lemon water as the last set of lunch orders left the kitchen. What a day it had been. The owners of Francine's, Mary and Jack, had said it was the busiest lunch crowd they ever had.

"Hot damn, woman, you sure can cook. I'm going to give you a raise and provide full benefits for you all."

"That's great, Jack. I appreciate it." Anna was relieved. She had wanted to stop by Doc Jones to ask how much she owed him for his medical services.

"Man, I'm so glad that went well. I was jumpy as spit on a hot skillet!" he exclaimed, and Anna laughed. Jack was full of crazy Texas slang, and she loved it.

"You laughing at me again, girl?" he teased, then winked. Anna shook her head, then turned toward the kitchen crew.

"Thanks, everyone. We worked well together our first day." She smiled.

"You bet ya, Anna. It was our pleasure," Miguel replied, and the others made similar comments.

Anna held her ribs, feeling the achiness increase the longer she stayed on her feet.

"How them ribs feeling, honey?" Mary asked as she joined them by the prep tables.

"I'm okay, just a bit tired."

"Well, why don't you call it a day. It's nearly four in the afternoon. I swear we will just have enough time for Cody to come in and cook all that food you prepped for the dinner crowd. It was an awesome lunch menu you prepared. Maybe when you're feeling better and all healed up, you'll be able to work the dinner shift as well," Mary stated then winked.

"That would be great. This place will be roaring with business. With cooking like Anna's, the Food Network will be stopping by to check Francine's out."

Mary laughed as she gave Jack a shove, then helped clean up the kitchen.

Anna finished up then grabbed her things.

"Can I use your phone? I need to call Stacy for a ride."

"I don't think you have to worry about that, honey. The sheriff checked in twenty minutes ago and said he'll meet ya here."

"Thanks, Mary." Anna smiled as she took her purse and headed outside to the main dining area.

Anna exited the doors, walking slowly. The more she walked, the more her ribs ached. She had been on her feet since nine in the morning, and now, she paid the price. She was certain if she had taken the time to pop some ibuprofen she would be feeling less achy.

"Hey, Anna, you feeling all right?" Stew asked as Anna held on to the counter for support.

She smiled, trying to brush off his concern.

"I'm good, just a bit tired."

"I would imagine so. I ain't never seen Francine's so crowded. You are an amazing cook," Stew stated as he walked closer to her. He was a little older than the Cantrells but just as attractive. She heard Beth, one of the waitresses, pining over him.

She smiled.

"That's nice of you to say." Anna took a seat near the counter. Stew stood next to her and a bit close for her comfort.

She looked toward the door, hoping that Wyatt would get there soon. She wanted to take a long, hot bath in their fancy tub.

"So, did you learn how to cook back in New York?" he asked, leaning toward her and brushing a finger over her arm.

"Yes. I worked at a bunch of places there." He was making her feel uncomfortable, and she sensed his attraction to her. This wasn't good.

"Is it true that you all are staying with Stacy and her men?" he asked, inching closer and touching her arm again.

"Hey, Stew, can you give me a little space? Are you writing a book or something?" she asked, and his eyebrows crinkled.

He put his hand on her knee, and when she tried to move, he put pressure there. Anna began to panic.

"I'm just wondering if you're fucking all the Cantrells, including Stacy's men."

"That's enough, Stew. If I were you, I'd hightail it outta here before the sheriff shows up. She's off limits, and unless you want to wind up in a heap of trouble, you'll stay clear," Jack stated as he approached the counter and pointed toward the door.

Stew stood up then placed his hand against Anna's cheek.

"Another time and another place, darling." He tipped his hat and headed toward the door.

Just then, the sheriff arrived.

"Stew."

"Sheriff."

Anna took a deep breath as she looked at Jack. She hoped he wouldn't say anything to Wyatt.

He gave her a wink, and Wyatt approached.

"He ain't causin' no trouble is he, Jack?" Wyatt asked as he tossed a look over his shoulder after Stew.

"Nahh…just shooten the shit, that's all."

He smiled.

"How's my woman?" he asked as he leaned down and gave her a kiss on the lips, pulling her from the seat. Anna cringed at the pain.

"She did real good. I'm sure you seen how crowded the joint was?"

"Sure did. They got tons of calls from people unable to find parking spots. Pretty interesting," Wyatt replied, then winked at Anna.

She blushed at his dimples. Unlike his brother, he had dimples in both cheeks, and even with the shadow of a beard, he looked lethal. She came to realize it only took until about noontime for Wyatt to start growing whiskers.

He helped her down, and she tried her hardest to cover the achiness.

Waving good-bye, they exited the restaurant, and he drove her home in the sheriff's truck.

* * * *

"You all tired, honey?" he asked as he squeezed her hand and held it against his thigh while he drove.

"Yes," she replied as she leaned her head back.

"I have a couple of more hours of work, and Ben and Charlie won't be in until supper time, so you can lie down if you want."

"I think I would love to take a long, hot bath in that delicious tub of yours."

"That sounds perfect. Don't y'all worry about dinner tonight. Stacy and the guys are throwing a little barbeque."

Anna smiled.

* * * *

Anna got the bath ready, adding some bath salts and bubbles Wyatt got from Stacy. He was so sweet, and she was certain she wasn't fooling him by hiding her sore ribs.

Slowly, she got undressed then carefully unwrapped the bandages. One glance in the mirror and she could see how red and bruised they were. The discoloration was fading, but at least she was healing. Today was the first day she was active all day and on her feet. She pushed it too far. Anna was certain after the bath that she would feel better.

She held the towel around her as she tested the water.

"Hey, Anna?"

She smiled as she heard Charlie's voice.

"I'm in here."

Charlie opened the door with a scowl on his face.

"Are you okay?"

She put her hands on her hips and nearly dropped the towel.

"Wyatt call you?"

"Should he have called me?"

Charlie walked closer and placed his hand against her cheek. She closed her eyes and leaned into his hand.

"You look tired."

"Mmmm."

"Let me take a look," he stated, and before she could protest, he pushed the towel away from her body.

He gently glided the palms of his hands over the bruising and around her waist. It was slow and felt so good.

"I think you overdid it today."

When she opened her mouth to argue, he placed his finger over her lips.

Charlie leaned down and kissed her lips then drew her naked body against his chest.

His hands roamed over her backside then squeezed before he tapped her cheeks.

"Get in the tub, and I'll help wash you."

Anna's stomach clenched at the thought of Charlie bathing her, especially when he tapped her ass that way. It was light and quick but still potent.

He helped her into the tub.

She released a relaxing sigh as the warmth of the water encased her aching body.

She leaned back and closed her eyes.

Damn, she was tired. But the longer she lay still, the better she began to feel.

Anna hadn't even heard Charlie until she sensed the water moving around her. When she opened her eyes, he was sinking into the tub to join her.

"Come here, baby. Let me help you relax," he whispered as he leaned back and gently pulled her toward him. As she moved across the tub, his erection hit her belly before she shifted so that her back wedged against his stomach. She settled in between as Charlie's legs encased her body.

* * * *

Charlie soaped up the washcloth and slowly began massaging Anna's arms. She had placed her hair up on top of her head in a wild style that would keep it dry during the bath. It left her neck open for his pleasure as he kissed along her collarbone. He liked the texture of her skin and the small freckles along the back of her neck right below the hairline.

He kissed each one as he cupped her breasts, massaging the soap over each nipple and areola.

"You have these three tiny freckles back here."

"I didn't know that," Anna moaned softly.

"It's like they're here just for me to feast on," he whispered, then nibbled along her neck. Anna giggled. The sound immediately tugged at his heart. She was so petite and feminine. He could crush her if he weren't careful, and the thought stirred such a protective feeling inside him. After the talk he had with Ben, he felt more protective. He didn't want Anna to suffer or to keep having nightmares because of New York. They had to get her to open up and share more details so Wyatt could investigate and make some calls. But pushing Anna wouldn't be smart.

He couldn't resist pulling on her nipples, tugging and rubbing, then tweaking, them. Her body arched at his touch, and his cock hardened against her back. He desired her all the time. Even on the ranch today, he missed her and wished she was nearby so he could check on her and of course make love to her.

He pushed his hand lower, reaching her belly button then lower between her thighs. Immediately, she parted for him, and he smiled triumphantly. His Anna wanted him as much as he wanted her.

When she parted her thighs and raised her knees above the water, his cock hardened.

Charlie pressed a finger into her channel, and Anna moaned. Her body arched, and her head tilted back until she reached his lips.

One look and that was it for both of them. Anna turned around slowly and straddled his hips. They sought the other's mouth and kissed then locked their bodies together.

She opened her eyes and began rubbing her hands over his chest hairs, tweaking his nipples before leaning forward to nibble on one.

"Oh, baby, that feels so good."

He felt her trace along his chest, and his stomach tightened. He hated his scars.

Rougher than he intended, he took her wrists to stop her from tracing the scars.

"Charlie, tell me how you got those?" Her soft voice eased his mind, but his fear of talking about the war after so many years made him uptight.

"Naw, baby, you don't want to hear all the gory details."

He released her wrist to rub a hand up her arm over her shoulder, then neck, to pull her down to him for a kiss.

She held her hands against his chest.

"Being a soldier is part of who you are, Charlie, and I want to know more about you."

He closed his eyes and released a sigh then pressed her head to his chest as he rubbed her back, then her backside, below the water.

"I served three tours, baby, in Afghanistan and a slew of other desert shitholes. I'm a Marine, honey. A medic and expert sniper by military standards."

Anna kissed his chest and rubbed a finger over one of his nipples.

"I guess you saw a lot of bad things then, huh, Charlie?"

He rubbed her back as the memories flashed through his mind.

"I did. I saw things I'll never talk about, Anna. It was a bad time in my life."

"You're a hero, Charlie."

"No, baby."

Anna sat up and cupped his face in her hands. Her eyes were glossy as she spoke.

"You are! Anyone who can serve his country to protect us here at home and ensure our freedom is a hero. You gave up your family, the safety and security of the United States of America, and a shitload of other sacrifices, so you deserve the title."

He smirked at her and the intensity of her tone.

"Too many bad things happened over there that I will never forget. I was in bad shape when I returned. I nearly lost my brothers and control of my own life."

Anna caressed his lower lip with her thumb before she spoke.

"Then we have a lot in common, Charlie."

"Yeah?"

She was silent a moment before she spoke. She was easy to talk to, and she truly empathized with his emotions and need to hold back details. He squeezed her a little tighter. He was falling in love with her.

He waited for her response.

"You're a survivor, Charlie, just like me."

It was an intense moment they shared. He pulled her mouth to his and kissed her softly. Before long, that kiss intensified, and all Charlie could think about was making love to his woman.

Charlie fisted his cock and aligned it with Anna's pussy as she lifted then took him fully inside of her, obviously needing him as well.

Their lips separated for a moment as her head fell back. Charlie took the opportunity to suck a nipple into his mouth as Anna rode him.

He let her start the pace while he rubbed his hands over her back then lower.

Their gazes locked again, and it was intense. So intense that Charlie felt his chest tighten and his heart soar with appreciation for the woman in his arms. There was no use fighting it, he and his brothers would do anything for the love of Anna.

Anna wrapped her arms around Charlie's neck and began licking and biting him then blowing in his ear. Her thrusts grew deeper and faster, causing water to spill over the edge of the tub. His cock was so damn hard he knew he was about to explode.

"Ride me, baby. Fuck me good," he ground out through gritted teeth as he squeezed and separated her ass cheeks.

Rubbing the crevice, then the puckered hole, had Anna fucking him harder, trying to get her release. Their lips locked again for an explosive kiss as he pushed one digit in and began to match the rhythm. They both found their release, moaning into the other's mouth then panting for air.

* * * *

Anna laid her head against Charlie's neck. Her whole body tingled, and her heart pounded against her chest.

"Who's going to clean this mess up?"

Both of them turned toward Ben, who now stood leaning against the bathroom door, naked.

Anna felt herself blush as she started to move away from Charlie.

He wouldn't let her and pulled her back against him.

"I'll take care of it, don't worry," Charlie stated then kissed Anna along her temple then forehead.

"It's hot in here, too. It's like a sauna," he complained as he headed toward them.

Ben reached out his hand for Anna to take it. She looked at Charlie and smiled.

"Later," he whispered.

"Later," she replied as Ben lifted her from the tub.

Ben pulled her to him, and she tilted her head all the way back to lock gazes with him.

"So, you overdid it, your ribs are sore, and then you ride Charlie in the tub? You're just asking for a spanking, ain't ya, baby," Ben teased as he gave her ass a light tap.

Anna hugged him, loving the feel of his muscles against her breasts.

"My turn, honey, but I have to shower first."

Ben held Anna's hand and headed into the shower.

* * * *

Charlie watched Anna cross the room. The sight of her bruises made him angry, and it had been very difficult to see them when they made love. If they ever got their hands on the assholes that hurt her, he would be sure to make them regret their actions. He had learned that Anna was a sweet and passionate young woman who had struggled through life just barely making ends meet. She had taken a chance in trusting him and his brothers, and he wouldn't let her regret that. She put up a tough front, but he knew she was hurting after the long hours on her feet today. She would have to learn to confide in them and not put her health in danger.

As he dried himself off then began cleaning up the mess around the floor, he smiled. He'd never made love to a woman in a bathtub. It was messy but well worth it.

As much as he wanted Anna to lean on him and his brothers, he was proud of Anna. She was strong, sexy, beautiful, and a fighter. He may have gone through war in Iraq, but Anna had been through a war right in her own home. Thank God she survived and made it to the Triple C.

* * * *

Anna was feeling pretty tired as she leaned against the shower wall and closed her eyes. Ben was washing the shampoo from his hair after they thoroughly cleansed one another's bodies. She smiled to herself. Ben was so sexual she couldn't help to think about the many women she was certain he'd had sex with. He was a player, but he was so damn cute and sexy, it didn't matter, and boy, did he know it. Whether he gave her a wink with his eye or nod of his head to come to him or to acknowledge him, she did it without a second thought. He had sex appeal, and he had a way of bringing out the sexual deviant in her. Never once would she of thought about anal sex. But with Ben, Charlie, and Wyatt, she wanted everything, and she wanted to give them anything she could.

Despite her crazy first day at work, she was feeling better about her life. Besides Stacy, she had her men to thank for that.

"What are you thinking about?" Ben asked as he pressed his body against hers.

Anna wrapped her arms around his neck, stood on her tiptoes to kiss his chin.

"I was thinking about you and your brothers and how lucky I am to have you."

Ben smiled, then squatted a little lower.

"How about I show you how lucky I feel to have you?"

He slowly slithered down her body, kissing her skin along the way.

"The bruises are looking better," he whispered as he kissed the tender flesh softly before moving lower.

Ben lifted her leg to balance on his knee as he squatted in front of her.

He had long, thick fingers, tanned from the sun and rough from all the hard work on the ranch. They expanded across her toned legs. The way those fingers stroked over her wet skin and the right amount of pressure and show of possession from his fingertips, made her feel needy. *Son of a bitch!* She really had it bad for Ben. She had it bad for all three of them. As if one wasn't enough, how the hell was she going to handle three?

She watched as his eyes, transfixed on her mound, peeked up to wink at her, the sexy bastard, before he stroked the folds with his fingers.

The warm water sprayed over them, adding to the feelings he drew from her.

Anna reached back to the wall for support as Ben placed his mouth against her.

Have mercy! He was deadly, and he had her there in seconds.

Ben plunged his tongue inside her folds and pumped his finger in and out of her, drawing more juices from her body.

"Sit back on the bench," he demanded as he lifted her rear, tilting her pussy closer to his mouth before she had a chance to move.

Anna forgot about the built-in bench. It was high, obviously custom made for the men because Ben had to help her onto it.

The bathroom was bigger than the bedroom. They could have a party in the shower, but that thought made her jealous.

Before she could ponder more about it, Ben rotated his finger then added another digit. When she was nice and wet, he lifted her and turned her body around to face the wall.

"Bend over the bench and rest your arms on it."

Anna did as he said and leaned forward, her ass pointed up in the air toward Ben and her forearms held her in position.

"Are you okay?" he asked as he leaned over her, reached between her legs, and pushed his fingers into her again.

"Yes." She panted.

He smoothed the palm of his hand over her ass cheeks then kissed and nuzzled her neck and shoulder.

She felt Ben remove his fingers, and without thought, she pushed back, needing him to touch her again. He chuckled next to her ear, and the vibrations sent chills over her skin.

"I'm gonna love fucking you from behind, Anna. Your ass is just the right size to hold, baby. You know…" He licked then nibbled her earlobe as he reached under her to pull on her nipples. His warm breath caressed her, and she closed her eyes, waiting for more.

"…I can be very demanding, and I have fantasies about the things I'd like to do with you. Right now, taking you from behind in this shower is only one of them." Her insides quaked at his words as moisture leaked from her mound.

"Oh, God," she moaned, leaning forward just as Ben pushed his cock against her entrance and rammed forward.

His growl echoed over the tile walls and through the room.

He took her from behind, thrusting forward as he pulled back on her hips.

In and out, he increased his speed as Anna held on to the slippery surface.

It felt so tight, and he was so deep this way, she couldn't catch her breath.

The sound of his balls slapping against her ass and the water sucking in between them made her feel wild, resilient, and oh so very sexy.

"Oh, yes, Ben, it feels so good." She moaned then pushed back against him.

"Slow down, or I'm gonna come."

"Isn't that the point?" she teased, sensing the frustration in his tone.

She jumped as she felt the smack to her ass.

"Keep it up, smart-ass, and watch what I do to you."

Her heart hammered inside her chest. Ben was so unpredictable, so...

She held her breath as she felt his finger push into her anus. Throwing her head back, she tried to breathe as the sensations of being full tore through her.

"Not so mouthy now, are ya?" he growled next to her ear and nibbled her earlobe.

Ben pushed in and out, rocking his hips and sending her closer to climax. When he pulled from her body, she wanted to protest, but then she felt his cock at her anus and waited in anticipation.

Slowly, he pushed through the tight rings and pressed fully up against her. His arm held her around the waist as he thrust slow and deep.

Anna opened her legs wider as Ben played with her clit and pressed a finger into her channel.

She screamed her release, unable to stand on shaky legs. Ben held her tight.

"I'm almost there, baby. Hold on for me," he barely got out as he pumped into her faster and faster. The water slapped between them, the temperature cooled, and she wanted more of him.

Anna pushed back, and Ben shoved forward, pressing her against the wall, and their fingers entwined.

He scraped his teeth across her neck and shoulder as he pumped fast and furious into her until he exploded inside her.

"Fuck! Damn, Anna!" he yelled, then panted, out of breath, but stayed inside her, gasping for air. It was a few moments before he pulled from her body, turned her around so fast she felt dizzy, then he squeezed her against his chest.

"That was fucking incredible," he panted, holding her beneath the cool spray of the water.

"Yeah...it sure was," she replied, kissing his chest, loving the feel of muscle beneath her lips.

She nibbled his nipple and lightly pulled on it.

Ben caressed her cheek and stared into her eyes when she lifted her eyes to him.

"One fantasy down and about a trillion more to go," he added, squeezing the globes of her ass before swiping his finger over the crevice.

Anna stirred in his arms.

Ben may just be the death of her...but what a way to go.

Chapter 13

It was a lovely, clear evening when Anna walked across the yard and over to Stacy, Max, and Eric's place. The men had headed over earlier, once they woke her from her much-needed nap. Anna felt pleasantly sore in all the right places, and amazingly, her ribs were not as achy.

She dressed in a short beige skirt that flared slightly at the bottom and brushed against her thighs a few inches above the knees. The white tank top accentuated her full breasts, along with her toned, defined arms. She felt cool and comfortable as the aroma of food traveled across the yard in her direction. Stacy's famous chicken wing appetizers were surely on the menu. Anna loved that smell of BBQ sauce, honey, lemon, and fresh thyme.

When she approached the yard, she smiled at the sight before her. Charlie, Wyatt, and Eric were standing by the custom-made outdoor kitchen preparing the grill for the food.

Ben was sitting in a chair with his legs wide, drinking a beer and talking with Max.

Stacy came onto the porch with a glass of iced tea and a bowl of chips.

"Hey, Anna!" she called, and all the men turned toward her as she climbed the steps.

"Hi!" She waved as Stacy put the items in her hands down and pulled Anna into a hug.

"How was the weekend?" Anna asked. Stacy giggled.

"It was fantastic. Since you didn't come back over last night, I'm assuming things went real well with the Cantrells?" Stacy teased, and Anna nodded.

"Yes!" Stacy exclaimed as she made a fist and pulled it to her hip at the same time.

Anna giggled.

"How are you feeling, baby?" Charlie asked as he wrapped his arms around her from behind, pulling her against his chest. Anna turned her head to the side and touched his cheek.

"I feel good."

"Well, you look real good," he whispered as he lightly pressed his erection against her backside.

Anna giggled.

"Come over here, sweetheart. Let me have a look at you." She looked toward Ben, who was curling his finger toward her, then back toward himself. Damn, he was a piece of work, and double damn, she went immediately to him after his command, but not before Charlie gave her a possessive tap to her behind. She swatted at his hand and tried to hide her embarrassment at the public display.

Stacy laughed as if reading Anna's mind and took a seat next to Max.

Ben looked her over, keeping his hands on her skirt as he had her turn around in front of him. He gave an approving nod of his head then winked at her.

Anna placed her hands on her hips, raised her eyebrows, and gave him a look right back.

"Oh, no, honey, I wouldn't be playing those types of games with Ben. You should know you're asking for trouble," Charlie added with a smirk then took a slug of beer from the bottle he held.

"Are you sassing me, girl?" Ben asked as he caressed her backside and pulled her to him so she would lose her balance.

"Ben!" she exclaimed as she fell forward, her cleavage practically wedged against his chin if she hadn't been fast enough to stop her fall by placing her hands on his shoulders.

He moved his feet between her feet and separated them, causing her to either lose her balance or shove her ass in the air and into Eric's face. The others had joined them on the porch.

Giving in, she fell against him in the large cushioned rocker.

Ben pulled her to him so she couldn't get up. His hand was around her waist and pressed against her back. His other hand was flat against her ass cheek for all to see.

Anna felt her cheeks redden and her temper rise.

"You better watch out, Ben, I think you've met your match," Eric egged Ben on as he laughed.

"Ben, let me up," she stated through clenched teeth. They were nose to nose.

Ben tightened his hold, making her breasts push up further and closer to his face.

She watched as his eyes looked down and the smile filled his face, dimples and all.

She struggled to get up and, in doing so, pushed her cleavage against his mouth.

Ben licked her skin, and the heat hit her cheeks, plus her panties.

"Damn you, Ben, this is completely inappropriate!" she reprimanded him, and Anna heard the chuckles, then the conversations continued around her. Now, no one was even paying attention.

Flustered, she locked gazes with Ben and gave him the evil eye. It didn't last but a few seconds. He was handsome and so darn sexy, she couldn't resist him. Fighting him didn't get him to stop, it just made him more determined to show he was the one in control. She tried a different tactic.

"Ben, honey, can you please let me up? My ribs are hurting."

He began to slowly release her, but stupid her smiled too soon. He realized she was lying and turned her in his arms so fast and so easily she didn't have a moment to escape.

Now, he held her like a baby across his lap, placed her head against his chest, and held his hand over her thighs.

There was no use in fighting him, so she gave up and joined the conversation with the others.

* * * *

Wyatt watched Anna as Ben, Max, and Charlie talked about the ranch, the animals, and their ideas for expanding the stables. Then they walked back out toward the grill to make sure everything was ready. It was just Wyatt, Ben, and Anna on the porch.

"Can you let me up now? I'd like to go help Stacy set the table."

"Give me some sugar first." Ben tilted his chin toward Anna and held her thighs so she couldn't move.

Anna released an exasperated sigh, and Wyatt laughed. Ben was a demanding man who didn't give two shits what anyone thought. He did what he wanted, when he wanted to, and that was it. It would be fun to see how he handled Anna. It was obvious that she appeased him to not cause a scene earlier, but something told him that she wasn't finished with Ben.

Anna gave Ben a quick, soft kiss then attempted to get up.

He held her still.

"I asked for sugar, honey."

Before Anna could respond, Ben pulled her toward him and kissed her long and wildly. Wyatt shook his head and laughed. When Ben finally released her, Anna's lips were swollen and red, and her eyes were filled with desire. His own cock throbbed against his jeans just from watching.

She slowly rose off of Ben's lap, and when she turned to leave, he rubbed his hand up her skirt and touched her. Anna swung around, apparently shocked at his brazenness.

"I'll be getting some of that later," he growled, then winked, and Anna huffed as she walked away.

Before she could get inside, Wyatt snaked an arm out and grabbed her around the waist to pull her to him.

"No hello for me, darling?" he whispered, then lightly caressed her swollen lips with his thumb.

Anna smiled at him before she hugged him.

He loved how she felt in his arms and against his chest. His nostrils filled with her scent and his groin ached to be inside of her.

When she pulled back, she smiled softly before standing on her tiptoes to kiss him. Wyatt moaned against her mouth as he gave her backside a squeeze and felt her up real quick before she pulled away. Anna swatted at his hand and straightened her skirt before she pulled completely away.

"Will you two stop it? Someone is going to see," she stated.

"Too late, honey."

Anna looked to the screen door of the house and saw Max standing there with a big smile on his face.

Anna shook her head and growled before opening the door and heading inside.

Wyatt laughed.

* * * *

"It appears some progress was made this weekend," Max stated as he joined Wyatt and Ben on the porch.

"Y'all could say that," Wyatt replied, then took another slug of beer.

Max chuckled.

"How 'bout you? Have a nice, romantic weekend with Stacy?" Wyatt asked.

He noticed that Max lit up immediately.

He stuck his hands in the front pockets of his jeans and started balancing forward and backward on the heels of his boots.

Something was up. Wyatt looked at his cousin sideways in challenge.

Max glanced toward Eric and Charlie.

"How them steaks coming along?" Max yelled.

"Just about done. The ladies ready with the table?"

"Yeah, we're ready! Let's move before it gets cold," Stacy ordered as she and Anna placed bowls on the table.

"That looks real good there, Stacy. I love potato salad," Ben added as he joined them near the table.

Wyatt observed the others pulling off the steaks then walking onto the porch with a tray of meat.

"Smells real good," Wyatt said, then watched Eric hug Stacy and smile wide next to her cheek.

"Let's eat," Stacy said, and everyone grabbed a seat around the table.

* * * *

Anna was enjoying the dinner when she noticed how attentive Eric and Max were being to Stacy. They kept adding more food to her plate, whispered to her so no one else could hear, but Stacy looked annoyed.

Apparently, Anna wasn't the only one who noticed.

"Okay. Spit it out. What in the hell is up with you three? You've been shoving food on the poor girl's plate and fussin' over her. It's driving her crazy."

Wyatt got everyone's attention with his statement, including Stacy, who began to laugh, nearly spitting the food in her mouth out.

"We're just making sure that she's eating enough and doesn't need anything," Max replied.

"Well, of course she needs fussin' over. She's pregnant!" Eric exclaimed, and the excitement filled the air. The men started asking questions about when Stacy found out, how far along was she, did they need any help with anything.

It was so wonderful and so exciting that Anna began to cry. This was a family where everyone cared about one another so much they were willing to sacrifice themselves for the other's needs. It was becoming clearer and clearer that reliability and trust was important in a family. Stacy was her family, and perhaps, just maybe, the men could be her family, too.

"Hey, baby, are you all right?" Charlie asked as he placed his arms around Anna's shoulders.

"I'm just fine," she blurted out.

"What is it, Anna?" Stacy asked.

"This is so perfect. I'm so happy for the three of you. Eric and Max, I know you're going to be fantastic fathers. I just know it."

Wyatt raised his glass and made a toast.

"I'd like to make a toast. To Max, Eric, and Stacy, may you be blessed with the first of many happy, healthy babies to add to the Cantrell family!" The men cheered, and Stacy laughed as she and Anna smiled at one another.

Chapter 14

"She doesn't trust us to tell us more." Ben couldn't help the upset in his own voice as he leaned against the porch railing over at their house. It was nearly midnight by the time they finished up dinner and celebrating over at Max and Eric's place.

Wyatt joined Ben and Charlie in mid-discussion.

"Anna's sound asleep. She exhausted herself today," he added before he took a seat on the single rocker next to Charlie and across from Ben.

"Poor thing. I'm worried that she's rushing the healing process. She should be here with us on the ranch where we can take care of her," Charlie added.

"She's independent. Don't you get that, Charlie?" Wyatt replied.

"That's because she's used to handling things on her own. We have to make her see that she doesn't have to anymore. I don't know about you guys, but I want it all with Anna. I want Anna's belly round with our baby and the house filled with kids we can enjoy and raise together. I, for one, have never wanted any commitments like that before." Ben stuck his hands in his pockets and looked embarrassed for making the statement.

"Shit, Ben. We'd be pissed at you if you didn't feel that way. I want the same thing, and so does Wyatt," Charlie replied, with a toss of his head toward Wyatt for confirmation.

Wyatt looked concerned.

"She's still keeping secrets from us," he stated, then rose from the chair.

"You mean about New York?" Ben asked.

"That, too. Something happened in the diner today."

"What?" both Charlie and Ben asked.

"When I came in to pick Anna up, I saw Stew next to her. He was real close, and I swear Anna looked nervous. I asked if everything was okay, and Jack said yeah. So did Anna, but Stew had gotten out of there real quick, if ya know what I mean?"

"Stew better stay away from her," Charlie whispered with his fists by his side.

"What makes you think something happened if Jack said nothing did?" Ben asked.

"I had a feeling he lied to me. I think for Anna's sake because he, too, noticed the way she responded. So I stopped by after I dropped Anna off here. Jack said Stew touched her and that before Stew could try something else, he intervened. Then I showed up."

"She didn't tell you any of this?" Ben asked, sounding angry.

Wyatt shook his head.

"We need to put a stop to this right away. She needs to know that we're here to protect her," Charlie added.

"I know, believe me, when I found out, I wanted to tear Stew a new one and throw Anna over my knee and teach her a lesson. She doesn't concern herself with her own safety. Her old man made her a victim in every sense of the word, and now, we need to teach her better," Wyatt stated.

"Well, if she withheld information about Stew, what about getting her to talk to us about New York so you can make some calls?" Charlie asked.

"That is what we need to do, but first, we have to resolve this issue of keeping information from us."

"Yeah, including knowing about Stacy and the baby," Ben added. Both Charlie and Wyatt stared at him as if asking, "What?"

"My woman is going to know that I'm in charge, and she better not withhold information of any kind to me. Including about friends, family, and especially herself." Ben huffed then turned toward the door.

"Whoa, Ben! Slow down, will ya? She's not like other women, Ben. She's been a victim of abuse all her life, and any attempt on our part to push her or be too forceful with her could be misconstrued as abusive."

"I wouldn't hurt her, Charlie! How dare you even suggest I would abuse her."

"Calm down, Ben, that's not what Charlie is saying. Just keep in mind her past and what little we know about Anna's life with her dad."

"Where are you going?" Wyatt asked Ben as Ben gave an exasperated exhale and headed inside.

"I'm going to bed, and first thing in the morning, Anna's gonna have some explaining to do."

* * * *

Her body felt heavy and weak, and she couldn't move. All she could do was lie there and watch the events unfold. Stacy looked so beautiful. She rubbed her hand over her slightly protruding belly as she leaned against the front porch. Her smile had Anna smiling as well. How wonderful that Stacy, Eric, and Max were going to have a baby. She thought about the men. They were nowhere in sight. As Anna slowly looked across the landscape around the ranch, she tried to move. She wanted to join Stacy, but she couldn't move. Suddenly, she heard the gunshot. One, two, three...Stacy's eyes widened in shock as blood covered her body. "The baby!" Anna screamed as two men walked over toward her, standing above her head.

"Did you really think we wouldn't find you? We'll kill everyone if we have to."

Anna was shaking and crying as Wyatt, Ben, and Charlie tried to wake her from another nightmare.

"Anna, honey, wake up. Come on, girl, wake up!" Ben exclaimed, holding her by her arms and giving her a little shake.

"This one is worse than last night's!" Wyatt exclaimed.

"Last night? This happened last night? Why didn't you say something?" Charlie asked, and then he caressed Anna's cheek.

"She said she didn't want to take the meds because they make her feel funny. We told her she had to take them tonight and that we'd be here for her," Wyatt added.

"She didn't take them again," Ben whispered in an angry voice as he tried to wake Anna. He was so damn angry with her.

Slowly, Anna began to come to again. The tears rolled down her cheeks, and she sobbed and held her stomach.

Wyatt tried to pull her to him, but she pushed him away. Charlie tried as well, and she did the same thing then tried to hurry off the bed.

Ben snagged an arm around her, pulling her across his lap.

"Where do you think you're going?" he demanded, holding her tightly against his chest.

Anna continued to cry and shove against him.

"Stop, Anna! I'm not letting you go. You have some explaining to do, and you're racking up points in the punishment department. You keep this shit up, and I'll turn that pretty little ass of yours pink."

Anna froze and stared at Ben. He kept his triumphant smile submerged when the sight of her fear and upset tore at his gut. No, he couldn't be weak around his Anna. She needed tough love, and he knew how to give it.

He watched her chest rise and fall. The T-shirt she wore was raised over her hips, her thighs exposed to them, and her nipples were hard and pressed against the white cotton. He assumed his brother Wyatt told her to forget about wearing any panties. She didn't need them, and they wouldn't stay on long.

He turned her legs so she straddled him, and he began to caress her skin and wipe the tears away.

"You're safe. It was just a bad dream," he whispered, and she closed her eyes and looked away. He felt her flinch as her eyes apparently made contact with Wyatt and Charlie.

Ben remained in control of the situation as he tapped her thigh, indicating for her to place her full attention on him.

"You didn't take the medicine again." It was a statement, not a question, and Anna seemed to get that. She pressed her hands against his chest and tried to escape. He held firm, and Wyatt took position behind her. Ben's legs hung over the bed, making Anna probably feel as if she could fall off his lap and onto the floor. She grabbed his shoulders but didn't press against him. She tried to keep space between them, which only pissed him off more. He was determined to possess her in every sense of the word. He wanted her to know that the four of them were one and that together they could defeat and conquer anything.

"Didn't you tell Wyatt and me that you would take the meds tonight after what happened last night?"

She swallowed hard and nodded.

"So you lied to us?" Her eyes widened, and he pulled her hips closer against him, spreading her legs and opening her pussy and ass to their touch.

His cock throbbed against the material of the boxers he wore, and all he wanted to do was use it to pound some sense into her. What a fucked-up thought, but she made him crazy with want and need.

"That will cost you a good spanking, Anna. Do you want to know why?"

"No. Why would you do that? I didn't mean to."

Ben cut her off by placing a finger gently over her lips. "We're here to protect you, care for you, and keep you safe. We trusted your word and that you would take the meds, and you didn't do it. You caused yourself unnecessary pain and heartache. Wyatt, Charlie, do you agree she needs to be punished?"

"No. They don't agree, you're crazy," she blurted out as Ben caressed her ass cheeks before dipping a finger inside her channel. He pressed up, and Anna pushed against his chest. Just as he thought, their little woman was hot and wet. He winked at his brothers' concerned faces, indicating what he found. They seemed to understand his silent signal and moved in to assist.

"She also put herself in danger at the restaurant today," Wyatt added as he ran his hands up her back, through to the base of her neck and hair, taking a handful to grip her, and slowly turned her head up toward him. Her chin was raised and her neck accessible as their gazes locked.

"I didn't," she whispered in a hoarse, raspy voice, then swallowed so loud they all could hear her.

"So, when Stew touched you at the restaurant, you told me right away that he did and that he scared you?" Wyatt asked, the anger immediately apparent in his tone. Ben growled and added another finger to her channel, pressing in and out.

"That's no good, Anna. You've been very bad," Charlie chimed in.

"The punishment is inevitable. Let's get started."

Anna moaned as Ben swiftly removed his fingers from her, Wyatt released his hold, and Charlie lifted her then turned her over Ben's knees. She squirmed, trying to get free, but Wyatt held her arms, taking off her T-shirt in the process, baring her flesh to all three of them. Charlie positioned her legs so her ass was slightly tilted up over Ben's lap and her feet were spread and to the floor.

Anna gasped in shock at their quickness until Ben pressed his hand to the crevice between her cheeks and massaged there. She stilled across his lap.

"This ass belongs to us. This body belongs to us, and we will ensure its safety and your health."

Smack!

Anna jumped, then shifted across his lap. Ben had to hold in the moan as her side rubbed against his tented boxers.

"Next time, you take the meds like a good girl and follow the doctor's orders."

Smack!

Another moan from Anna.

"Fucking beautiful. I can see her cream dripping down her thighs," Charlie stated, then rubbed a finger over the wetness below and brought it up toward the crevice between two very pink cheeks. He pushed his finger over the puckered hole then in.

"Oh!" Anna moaned and moved further across Ben's lap before grabbing on to Wyatt's leg for support.

With Charlie's finger pushing in and out of her hole, Ben continued to punish Anna.

"You will learn to not keep secrets from your men. You knew about the baby and didn't tell us either." *Smack!*

Charlie and Wyatt looked at him as if he were nuts for punishing her for that, but then he shrugged his shoulders and smirked. It was obvious he was enjoying himself.

He caressed her cheeks then pushed a finger inside her pussy as Charlie continued the in-out motion into her ass.

She bucked and moaned across his lap then screamed her release. Both men removed their fingers.

Smack!

Ben rubbed his hands across her rosy cheeks while Anna panted for air.

* * * *

Wyatt pulled her off of Ben and lifted her up against his chest. She straddled his waist, and he grabbed a handful of hair at the nape of her neck and gently pulled back. He covered her mouth with his own, devouring her moans. He felt Anna's hands then fingernails scrape along his arms and chest.

"Hold on to me," he growled after releasing her lips. She did as he told her, and Anna began biting, sucking, and nibbling on his neck while holding on to him.

Wyatt pushed his boxers off and fell to the bed with Anna on top.

* * * *

She should be pissed, but instead, Anna never felt more compelled to dominate and devour. Her men may be able to smack her ass and make her come, but she would be damned if they thought she was going to just let them have all the fun.

Ben thought he was in control, but he wasn't. They had awoken a hidden side of Anna she never knew existed. The sound of their naughty mouths as they seduced her body and soul didn't make her cringe, it made her wanton. She felt independent, powerful like a sex goddess on a mission to conquer her men's bodies and make them need her just as much as she needed them, if not more.

She licked across Wyatt's skin, rubbed her very sensitive breasts against his muscular chest and lifted her ass in the air toward the audience behind her.

She felt sexy and on a mission, but Wyatt wasn't a man to be controlled. His knees bent at the edge of the bed, and he spread his legs, causing Anna's thighs to open wider to everyone's viewing. She sucked in a breath as the cool air collided with her slit then refocused on her objective to get Wyatt to come before she did.

Locking her ankles around where Wyatt's knees bent for support, she lifted her ass in the air, pressed her breasts against his stomach, and licked her way to his large, hard cock.

Wyatt tried to grab for her hair but froze the second she took his length deep into her throat.

"Oh, fuck, baby!" he yelled as Ben and Charlie made similar comments behind her.

The feel of two sets of hands caressing her ass and cunt sent waves of passion igniting through her, but she held on, refusing to come before Wyatt and maybe before Charlie and Ben as well.

Anna moaned and sucked up and down, licking, nibbling while simultaneously releasing his cock to run between her large cleavage. She was blessed with an abundant chest, and damn it, she was going to use her assets to tame her cowboy.

"Oh, fuck, Anna, where the hell did you learn to do that!" he yelled.

Smack!

Anna jerked back, surprised at the hit to her ass cheek. Who did that?

Ben leaned over her shoulder as he pressed a finger to her anus.

"I know what you're doing, but it ain't gonna work," he whispered then pumped his finger in and out of her.

When Charlie reached underneath her and Wyatt to press two fingers into her channel, she nearly came.

"It's on!" she stated to herself then pulled Wyatt's cock into her mouth and sucked like she never would taste heaven again.

Wyatt's roar filled the room as he crashed and burned while she slurped and cleaned him from balls to tip.

One down, two to go.

Wyatt lay there with his arm across his eyes, breathing rapidly, and looked very content.

* * * *

Before Anna could celebrate, Ben lifted her off of Wyatt.

He placed her on the bed on all fours, grabbed her by the hips, and plunged into her from behind in all of about two seconds flat. She screamed, shocked against the invasion, but that didn't stop Ben from claiming her in the most dominant way a man could.

She had pissed him off and now faced his wrath. Oh, Lord, this was not going to be easy. Anna tried to push back to counter his thrusts, but it landed her a slap to her ass and a yank on her nipples. She felt herself caving in.

As she gasped for air, Charlie grabbed her hair and gently pulled her mouth closer to his cock that he held in his fist.

"Suck it!" Ben growled, still keeping his intense pace.

Her knees felt wobbly, and her entire insides felt enflamed, but she took a deep breath then went in for her second kill.

Charlie moaned then softened his hold. *Oh, yeah…he was as good as done.*

Confidently, she focused her attention on Charlie, which seemed to enrage Ben. She guessed he didn't like the taste of his own medicine.

Anna did exactly to Charlie as she did to Wyatt. Ben wrapped an arm around her waist and shoved in deep while supporting her weight. She took that moment to lift her hand and massage Charlie's sack while sucking and humming, and all hell broke loose.

Charlie grabbed her by the hair and increased his speed.

"Fuck, I'm gonna come!" Charlie yelled, then exploded inside Anna's mouth.

As she sucked and licked him clean, Ben pulled out from her channel and moved higher. She felt him touch her anus then his cock pushed through, while his fingers pushed into her channel.

"Oh, God!" she screamed as Ben took complete control of the situation and fucked her like there was no tomorrow.

She was going to lose. There was no way she would make it.

Wyatt shoved underneath her as Ben lifted her from around the waist, and Wyatt's cock replaced Ben's fingers.

They immediately fell into a rhythm. One cock pressed in while the other pressed out, then both were in together, and that was it. She screamed her release as the sweat dripped from her hairline, and she struggled to catch her breath as both Wyatt and Ben exploded inside her during a frenzy of thrusts.

Slowly, they pulled from her body, and Anna collapsed onto the bed.

* * * *

"Do you think we were too rough with her this morning?" Charlie asked then covered his mouth to yawn.

Ben laughed then stretched out against the wooden post with his arms crossed in front of him.

"Nah…she needed to be taught a lesson," he added with a smirk.

"Yeah, well, in that department, Wyatt and I failed. That fucking mouth of hers, damn, I get all hard just thinking about it." Charlie shifted his weight.

"You don't have to tell me. The woman is a natural seductress, and she knows it. Played you two like a fiddle."

"Fuck, yeah. I don't give a shit what you say. She can do what she wants to me."

"Hey, what are you two doing taking a break. It ain't even ten yet." Max exclaimed as he joined them by the fence.

"Just a little tired this morning, cuz, we'll get our work done," Ben replied sarcastically.

"Long night, huh?" Max asked then smirked.

"The best kind," Charlie replied, and then they all chuckled.

* * * *

"Sheriff Cantrell, I have a call for you from a Detective Phillips, New York City Police Department," Sally the secretary stated, interrupting Wyatt's conversation with Deputy Ted Bulkin.

Wyatt was immediately concerned, and his gut got all twisted inside. He thought about Anna.

Wyatt went into his office and took the call.

"This is Sheriff Cantrell. How may I help you?"

"Good morning, Sheriff. I'm Detective Bulking. I am trying to locate a Miss Anna Parker, the daughter of Hank Parker. A previous employer gave me a town and a first name of a close friend of Miss Parker's. I know it's not much, but the woman's name is Stacy."

"If you don't mind me asking, Detective, what is all this about? Why are you trying to locate this woman?"

"There's an ongoing investigation into her disappearance, and simultaneously, this is a death notification, Sheriff. I'm trying to locate Miss Parker to let her know that her father is dead."

"Dead? How did that happen?"

"Well, that's what we'd like to talk to Miss Parker about. She was the last person known to be seen with him. She disappeared, leaving no notice to her job, all her stuff is at the apartment, which was ransacked, and no one has been able to locate her. We did find a record of this woman Stacy and a plane ticket purchased three weeks ago with cash and a direct flight to Texas."

Wyatt's stomach clenched. Did this detective think that Anna killed her own father?

"Well, Detective, are you investigating this woman as a possible suspect?"

"We're covering all our bases, though I can tell you that a woman fitting her description bought a bus ticket to your town and that woman was described as having bruises. We're trying to get to the bottom of this."

"Well, you called the right place, Detective. I think there're a few things we need to discuss."

With that, Wyatt told the detective what he knew about Anna, and the detective shared his information about the murder investigation. By the end of the call, Wyatt found out that there was evidence left behind at the crime scene that identified two known felons working in an organized crime syndicate.

* * * *

"Hey, Ben, we got ourselves a situation," Wyatt stated as he called his brother on the cell phone. Since getting the call from the city, he'd sat in his patrol car a block away from the diner watching every patron that entered and exited. He had the detective from the city fax over pictures of the two thugs believed to have assaulted and killed Anna's father. The detective needed Anna to identify the two men as the ones who attacked her in order for her to press charges and testify to them hustling her father for a debt he owed. The detective also informed him about how ruthless and dangerous these two men were.

"What situation is that?" Ben asked.

He explained about the phone call.

"Son of a bitch! Did you check on her? Is she still there?"

"Yes, I'm sitting outside of the drug store. I've got the fliers with the assholes' pictures on it. Sally's making copies and distributing them around the department. I don't even want to think about how Anna is going to react to the news. It's way worse than I thought."

"How so, Wyatt? You better damn well tell me everything."

"Calm down, Ben. I won't withhold information from you or Charlie. I also think we need to make Max, Eric, and the workers on the ranch know what's happening. I'll bring home papers with these thugs' photos on them to distribute to the workers."

"So, tell me about these two assholes. Charlie is right here, so I'm going to put you on speaker."

"They're both felons, long criminal records and organized crime."

"Organized crime? You mean like Al Capone organized crime?" Charlie asked.

"More like John Gotti. Yes. They're connected to the Burgolino family, which, from the detective's perspective, is pretty well organized. They're on the FBI watchlist and are involved in everything from drug dealing, bribes, weapons, prostitution, and…and illegal sex slave business."

"Fuck!" Ben yelled.

"I know. I don't even want to think about what could have happened to Anna. Thank God she's as tough as she is."

"I want her here now. Go fucking grab her out of that restaurant and bring her here, Wyatt, or Charlie and I will do it ourselves."

"Calm down, Ben. How is that supposed to make Anna feel? I don't even know how she'll react to the news about her father's murder. Don't you think that's going to be enough for her to deal with? If I, or you, go into the restaurant making demands and forcing her to leave, she could panic and run clear out of town the first chance she gets."

"She wouldn't do that. You don't think she would do that, do you?" Charlie asked.

They were all silent.

Wyatt finally spoke. "Anna should be finished by three this afternoon or so. Let's just plan on making everyone aware of the situation, break the news about her dad to Anna, then find out more about what happened in New York. Initially, the detective thought she was involved with the murder."

"What?" both Charlie and Ben asked in unison.

"I explained her side as we know it, and he wants her to confirm the story and identify the suspects as the ones that threatened her and tried to abduct her."

"Her nightmares are going to get worse," Charlie whispered.

"We'll make her take the meds, and we'll help her get through how they make her feel. We'll talk more later tonight once Anna settles down for the night."

"I can't believe this is happening. I want her in my arms, with us, right now," Ben stated.

"Me, too."

"I wish I could get her out of there, but it will make matters worse. Let's just spread the word. It's a small town, and the people of Pearl are family. They'll pull together. They already like Anna a lot. You should see how crowded the restaurant is. I'll touch base later."

Wyatt leaned back and watched the restaurant from afar. Everything the detective told Wyatt played out in his head. He didn't want his Anna to suffer any more. He wanted her future to be with them, married, raising a family and expanding the ranch and the Cantrell name. No fucking mobsters from New York were going to take those dreams away from them.

* * * *

While Anna finished cleaning up the kitchen and preparing for the following day, Wyatt explained things to Jack.

"We'll keep our eyes opened, Wyatt. Ain't no fucking assholes going to come into Pearl and mess with one of our own. I can't believe they tried to take her and…" Jack shook his head.

Wyatt was happy with the response from Jack and the fact that the town's people thought of Anna as part of Pearl.

"I know, Jack. My brothers and I try not to think about what could have happened to her. She needs our protection. I know I can count on you, just like when you told me about Stew."

"Don't you worry about Stew. Ben met up with him this morning at the lumberyard. Set him straight, if you know what I mean. I swear, that brother of yours is one tough son of a bitch. Between him, Charlie, and you, only a man with a death wish would want to mess with any of ya."

"I'll have to find out what my brother did."

"Okay, Sheriff, I'm all set," Anna stated as she interrupted their conversation and headed straight toward them.

The sheriff nodded toward Jack, and they said good-bye.

As soon as Wyatt had Anna near the sheriff's patrol truck, he pulled her into his arms and kissed her. He rubbed his hands over her body possessively and to ensure she was in one piece. It was a foolish reaction, but he loved her. Fuck! Where the hell did those words come from?

He released her lips and swallowed the lump in his throat.

Anna appeared breathless but still in his arms.

"I missed you, darling," he whispered.

"I think I like being missed," she replied, then smiled. She was innocent and beautiful in every way. His heart pounded against his chest. He would wait until later to tell her about her father. Ben and Charlie would want to be there, as well as Stacy.

"Let's go, honey. I'm sure Ben and Charlie missed you, too."

Chapter 15

As Wyatt pulled the sheriff's truck in front of the house, Anna saw Ben standing by the barn talking to a few workers. He turned towards Anna and Wyatt and waved.

"I'll get out here and go see Ben before I take a shower."

"Okay, honey. I'll be back in a little while," Wyatt replied then leaned across the seat to kiss her. Anna placed her hand against Wyatt's cheek, loving the feel of his light whiskers.

He released her lips, and they smiled before she exited the truck.

Waving good-bye to Wyatt, she hurried over to meet Ben.

She missed him just like she missed Charlie. It was crazy how concerned she was originally about being in a ménage relationship. She didn't think she had enough in her to be with three men at once. It was different than anything she had ever heard of before, and she was glad she had held on to her virginity. She could have made a mistake and just had sex just to have it.

She slowed her pace as Ben continued to talk to the men. She didn't want to interrupt, and he held his hand up, indicating to give him a minute. She froze in place then slowly walked to the right of them and the horse corral. She noticed the cowboys glance her way as they folded up pieces of paper, placing them in their pockets.

Anna looked out at the horses. It was beautiful here, and she loved everything about Pearl. She didn't want to think about her past anymore. She didn't want the nightmares and the bad memories to rule her life and weaken her. There was a sense of newfound strength inside her growing stronger every day. She knew where that stemmed from. Between arriving on the Triple C, and having the initial support from Stacy, Max, and Eric she was beginning her healing process. When she met Charlie that first night on the ranch, with his concerned facial expression and ability to care for her, she knew he was special she just had to release her fear and trust again. She had immediately trusted him. Why else would she have allowed a complete stranger to see her wounds and hold her in his arms while she processed through another bout of nightmares?

Then there was Ben. Initially, she wasn't certain about his personality. He had that wild, confident look about him. Like he could be narcissistic without coming across narcissistic, but instead, he was just confident and sexy. He made her laugh now, but she recalled his explicit language initially made her nervous and embarrassed. Boy, had he changed her. Now, she loved it when he talked dirty to her, and she was beginning to give him some of his own naughty verbal medicine.

She smiled. Boy, did she get them all good last night. The look on Wyatt's face was enough to make her blush right now. Why she started the game of making them come before her she had no idea. It was how they made her feel. She wasn't so shy and unwilling to experiment with them. She loved them.

Her heart pounded in her chest.

"Hey, darling!" Ben exclaimed, catching her off guard. She turned to him with a huge smile on her face and practically jumped into his arms.

"Whoa! I am liking this kind of welcome," he exclaimed, chuckling.

She held him tight, with her arms around his neck before she squeezed him to her.

"I missed you, Ben."

"I missed you, too."

He squeezed her back then let her feet back on the ground before he held her from behind, and they looked out at the scenery together.

She loved the feel of his strong arms. He was built trimmer than Wyatt and similar to Charlie. The three Cantrells were in great physical condition.

Ben kissed her neck as he held her around the waist.

"You smell good."

"You must be hungry," she retorted, teasing him. She reeked of fries, burgers, and onions. Her specialty burgers were a huge hit at Francine's.

He chuckled.

"I'm hungry all right." He licked her neck, and she rolled her head back until he claimed her lips in a sensual kiss.

"Mmmm…honey, I could eat you up," Ben replied after releasing her lips.

"I smell like burgers, that's why."

"You always smell good to me and ready to nibble on."

She began to laugh and pull away from Ben as he nibbled her neck a little harder and tickled her.

She laughed as he held her hands at a distance, keeping her from running off.

"Let me go take a shower before Wyatt and Charlie get here. Then I can make some dinner."

He pulled her against his chest and kissed her again.

When he released her lips, he smiled.

"You might just get you some company in that shower, darling!" he exclaimed as he released her. She glanced down towards the crotch of his jeans, and her heart hammered in her chest.

"You want some of that, baby? Go on up, and get started. I'll be up in a few," he retorted, all sexy and confident as usual. She felt all giddy inside as she shook her head and ran towards the house, lighthearted and happy as could be.

Anna was upstairs taking a shower when she heard Ben and Charlie call her name.

"I'm in the shower!" she exclaimed as she let the warm water caress her muscles. It had been another crazy busy day at the restaurant. Considering she was around so much food, she felt kind of hungry. Or maybe it was a different kind of hunger she felt once Ben got a hold of her outside by the horse corral. Boy, was that man a piece of work.

She wondered what the guys had planned for dinner. Maybe she would cook for them tonight. She had wanted to mention it this morning, but things got a little out of hand. She smiled as she remembered the way they made love to her and the spanking. Damn, there was something seriously wrong with her. She should be afraid of that type of control, but there was definitely a difference between the way they spanked her and the way she had been abused. It wasn't like her father had hit her all the time. Sometimes his insults and hurtful comments about her looks or the way she did something hurt worse than getting hit. She swallowed hard, then turned off the shower.

When she looked up, both Ben and Charlie stood there waiting for her. Ben held a large towel open, and she went right to him.

He wrapped the warm, fluffy towel around her body and hugged her close. She closed her eyes and absorbed the love he gave.

Ben immediately held her from behind and nuzzled her neck after pushing aside the wet strands of hair.

"We missed you," Charlie stated, but Ben just squeezed her tight.

She got a little funny feeling in her belly but dismissed it. It was probably from the thoughts in the shower.

Anna stepped away and smiled.

"I missed you, too."

"Let me get dressed then I can start cooking dinner. Are you guys almost finished with work?"

They eyed one another, and Anna got that funny feeling again.

"We took out some chicken this morning. We can just throw it on the grill with some barbeque sauce and have it on rolls with lettuce and tomatoes. Is that good?" Charlie asked.

"I guess so, if that's what you want."

Anna felt like they didn't want her in their kitchen. Was that too intimate? Had she read their feelings and intentions wrong? Maybe they did just want to share her for a while then move on? Her head began to ache at the thoughts.

As she walked toward the bedroom, Ben grabbed her arm.

"What's wrong?"

"Nothing."

"Don't give me a 'nothing'. Didn't you learn anything after your punishment this morning?" Ben teased, squeezing her arm a little tighter.

She lowered her eyes. She didn't want to admit her fears, and she didn't want to hear him say that they weren't serious about her. It would hurt so much.

She felt his fingertips under her chin as he tilted her face up toward him. Charlie stood beside Ben with his hands on his waist, and his eyebrows crinkled. She began nibbling her bottom lip.

A gentle brush of the lips from Ben's thumb stopped the nibbling.

"What's wrong?"

"I understand, it's okay, Ben, I just assumed too much. Relationships are new to me."

"What are you talking about?"

"I understand that you don't want me in your kitchen. That's too personal, and we've just started…seeing one another."

"What makes you say that?" Charlie asked.

"You don't want me to cook for you. You don't want me in your kitchen and making myself at home. I understand."

"No, Anna, you don't. You got it all wrong. We didn't want you to feel you had to cook for us after cooking all day at the restaurant.

And where the hell did you get some ridiculous idea that this relationship isn't serious?" Ben demanded to know.

"We want you here. We want you everywhere," Charlie added as he moved closer to her.

His eyes looked darker suddenly, and it warmed her inside.

"We're looking forward to fucking you in every room in this house. In the kitchen, on the table, against the door…fucking everywhere." Ben pulled her close and kissed her before she could respond.

A second later, she felt the towel loosen around her body.

"I say we show her how much we want her in our home," Charlie whispered against her ear as he caressed her shoulders and nibbled on her collarbone.

Anna rolled her head back against Charlie's shoulder as Ben knelt down in front of her. He placed her foot on his thigh and spread her legs before blowing warm air against her folds.

"Just a little appetizer before dinner, baby," Ben whispered as he licked her folds and began to feast on her.

It was merely a matter of minutes before Anna moaned her release while holding Ben against her with his mouth still latched on.

The sound of their cell phones ringing, then beeping, put an end to the feast.

They each hugged her, patted and caressed her bottom, and told her to come downstairs for supper because Wyatt was on his way.

Slowly, and still feeling a bit dazed, Anna began to dress.

* * * *

"We've been watching this place for twenty-four hours. What the fuck are we waiting for?" Vinny whispered, agitated that they were stuck out in the middle of a field with binoculars.

"You have to have patience. Am I the only one who saw over a dozen big ass cowboys and the fucking town sheriff? He don't look like no hillbilly to me," Jake replied as he lifted the binoculars again.

"Fuck this shit! As soon as she's alone and we get a chance to grab her, let's do it and get the fuck out of here. I'm all congested from the fields, and these fucking hick clothes are putting a damper on my style. How do they wear this fucking thermal plaid shit?"

Jake laughed.

"You're congested because your nose is used to city air not fresh country air. It's probably better for your health to live out here."

"With the smell of cow shit? I don't fucking think so."

"Those men are always around her. We should wait until night when the workers are in their bunk houses or grab her at the restaurant."

"The restaurant is too risky unless we enter through the back, light up the place with some gunfire, grab her, then speed out of town. There're only three deputies. We could take out the tires on their vehicles first."

"That's a fucking stupid idea. The town has people everywhere. It's like fucking Mayberry and shit. No. We take her here."

"Those three men, including the sheriff, are fucking her, I just know it."

"This is definitely a fucked-up town. We've seen a few women with more than one man. It's a twist on polygamy."

"It's twisted, period. I wouldn't let another man fuck my wife."

"You're so full of shit. You just offered Marcus Anna, and me, if I wanted."

"She's not my fucking wife. I was going to use her body to get back the money."

"Bull fucking shit! As soon as you have the chance, you're fucking her and keeping her for yourself. I've known you since fucking grade school. Now shut the fuck up, and use those two hundred fucking dollar binoculars you insisted on getting and hope tonight is the night. I want to get back to New York."

Chapter 16

It was after seven in the evening. They had finished dinner and were sitting on the porch.

Stacy, Eric, and Ben had joined at Wyatt's request. The sun had set, and the darkness filled the yard except for the soft glow of the lampposts that stood on the corners of Eric and Max's house.

Stacy talked about plans for the nursery, and Anna made suggestions for colors and themes. They were giggling and enjoying the moment, and Wyatt felt sick to his stomach being the bearer of bad news.

As the conversation quieted down, Wyatt took the moment to speak. Everyone was silent.

"Anna, I received a call today at work."

Anna and her beautiful, big, brown eyes focused on his every word. He loved her, damn it, and this sucked.

"It was from a detective in New York."

"What?"

He watched her glance around at everyone's faces, and instantly, she knew something was up. She clasped her hands on her lap and swallowed hard.

"It's about your father."

Anna sat frozen in place as Wyatt explained everything the detective had told him. She only widened her eyes once when he explained that she initially was a suspect in his murder, but then he was quick to explain how he made the detectives understand the true story. When he was finished overloading her with the information, she still showed no emotion or response.

Stacy caressed her hands, and Anna flinched at the contact.

"Anna, honey, talk to us," Stacy asked, but Anna didn't respond.

"Baby?" Charlie stated then Anna looked at each of them.

"If you'll excuse me. I need a few minutes alone," she said then stood up.

"I'll come with you," Ben stated, rising from his seat.

Anna put up her hand to stop him.

"No. I need a few minutes…please?" Then she walked toward the porch door and headed across the yard into the night.

The sound of the door slamming seemed to echo in the quiet night.

* * * *

"Fuck! I don't think she should be alone." Charlie expressed his concern as he stood and began pacing.

"She needs a few minutes, Charlie. It's understandable," Wyatt replied.

"She showed no real reaction. I don't know what thoughts were going through her head, but she looked so numb," Ben added.

"I think she's confused. It was only recently she learned that her father didn't really love her. She had spent years taking care of him and providing for them. Now, he's been killed, and she probably doesn't know whether she should be happy or sad," Stacy added as she stood up.

Everyone was silent.

"Let's give her a few minutes then I'll go talk to her," Stacy replied, and the men agreed.

* * * *

Anna walked a good distance before she realized just how far she had walked. The river where she had told Stacy her story had already held special meaning for her. The moonlight glowed above, casting some light across the fresh, sparkling water.

She hugged herself, waiting for the tears to flow, but they never came.

She couldn't shed a tear for the man who broke her heart and nearly ruined her faith in ever being able to trust. Hank Parker was a mean old son of a bitch. He had been abusive, dishonest, and didn't give a damn whether she lived or died just as long as she provided money. He gave her away the first chance he had.

Yet, one small part of her felt empty. Perhaps it was because her father was the last living relative she had. That thought brought tears to her eyes.

But then she thought about Stacy and the men. If it weren't for her relationship with Stacy, she would have been all alone out there and never would have met Wyatt, Charlie, and Ben.

A smile formed on her lips as she wiped the stray tears and took a deep breath.

Her senses kicked in after a moment, and she could have sworn she smelled men's aftershave.

Another quick inhale and her chest tightened. It was the same cologne as the man from New York. She looked around, didn't hear a sound, and the smell seemed to disappear.

A few seconds passed of her listening to her own heartbeat and the sounds of nature around her when she finally relaxed. It was just her imagination playing tricks on her. Her father was dead, and her past life in New York was over officially.

She was going to be just fine. She had the men, a new job, a place to live, and she was in love. She had been in love the moment she allowed herself to get to know each of her men. She had known it and pushed it off as inexperience and the fact that her men were cowboys. They were gorgeous, sexy, and rugged. Never mind demanding, especially in the bedroom.

"Anna!"

She heard Stacy calling for her in the distance. Taking a deep breath to answer, she turned just as a large, solid hand covered her mouth while another wrapped around her waist.

Instantly, she knew it wasn't one of her men.

* * * *

"Hey, gorgeous. We've been waiting for you," he whispered against her ear as he rubbed his erection against her back. She instantly smelled the cologne. It was real, and he was here to take her back.

Anna was so frightened. She remembered that voice. How did they find her?

She struggled in his arms, and he tightened his hold. She heard Stacy getting closer. Oh, God, no! The baby. She couldn't let them hurt her.

"Your cute little girlfriend is coming this way. Maybe my partner should grab her for himself. She had a nice set on her, too," he whispered.

Anna shook her head.

"No? You don't want us to take her, too? Then cooperate and stay quiet, or she's dead."

Anna froze in place, trying to let him know that she agreed to his terms.

"Man, I'd love to fuck you right here against this tree. If the bitch wasn't so close, I'd do it. I guess I can hold off a little longer," he stated as he began walking her farther away from where Stacy was.

His partner stayed close. They didn't use flashlights, which made Anna think that they knew where they were going and had been watching her.

She was so scared. But she needed to focus on Stacy's safety. As long as she kept these men away from Stacy then she could deal with getting away from them herself as soon as she had the chance.

Way in the distance, she heard Wyatt's voice, then Ben and the others. They were searching for her. Were they close enough to Stacy to protect her? She couldn't take the chance that they weren't. Her heart continued to pound against her chest. She was so scared, but she worried about Stacy and the baby, so she didn't fight them.

They walked through a heavily dense area of bushes and trees before a clearing. Anna hadn't been this far out on the property, so she had no idea where they were or how far away from the house or main road.

"We better move fast, Vinny. Marcus warned us about leaving too many dead bodies around."

"We're almost in the clear. You drive, so my woman and me can get to know one another better," he stated then ran his hands over her thigh and between her legs. Anna shoved his hand away then sprang free, but before she could get away, his partner grabbed her by the hair, pulling her back. She screamed at the pain.

Vinny smacked her across the mouth, sending her flying to the dirt.

* * * *

"Stacy, did you find her?" Eric asked as he caught up to her by the river, along with Max.

"No. Damn it, where could she have gone?" Stacy asked, now very concerned.

"Hey, any sign of her?" Charlie approached, along with Wyatt and Ben.

They shook their heads.

Wyatt started looking around the area and by the river.

"She wouldn't just run off. I don't like the feeling I have," Stacy stated as Eric pulled her to him.

"Wait, listen…do you hear that?" Charlie asked.

Everyone quieted down.

"That sounded like a scream," Ben replied, and they all began running toward the fields.

"We'll grab the truck!" Eric stated, still holding Stacy's hand. Max ran ahead to get the keys to the truck.

"Motherfucker! We should have never let her leave!" Ben yelled.

"Let's just get to her. Damn it, I wish I had a flashlight," Charlie stated as they ran as quickly as they could through the trees.

* * * *

Vinny pulled Anna up off the ground and shoved her against the car. She cringed in pain as the metal made contact with her back.

"You little bitch! Stop trying to run. You're mine, and there's no getting out of it!" Vinny struck her again, but across the cheek instead of the mouth. She felt the pain, but something else came over her. She was angry and so scared, but she didn't want to leave. She didn't want them to win and take her away from Charlie, Ben, and Wyatt.

"I'm not yours! I won't leave here with you," she screamed.

Vinny smirked as Jake yelled for him to get into the car.

Vinny grabbed her by the hair, and she kicked and screamed, fighting him with all she had. She used her fingernails and felt them rip as they scratched deeply into his skin. She screamed at the top of her lungs as he threw her into the backseat of the car.

Reaching above her, she grabbed for the door handle to try and escape, but he slammed her in the stomach. She cried out, still trying to fight him and grab for the handle.

Somehow, she got it open as he ripped the shirt from her body, and she fell to the ground headfirst.

Her cheek and temple hit the ground hard, stunning her a second, before someone grabbed her from the ground and pulled her up.

As it registered in her head that Jake had grabbed her, he slammed her head forward and into the metal frame of the door.

* * * *

"I hear her, there, over there. Fuck, what are they doing to her?" Charlie stated, but they were running so fast, listening to her screams, and the adrenaline was flowing.

Wyatt reached the clearing first and growled as he saw a man bang Anna's head against the car. She looked like a rag doll as she fell to the ground.

"Get away from her!" Wyatt roared as he attacked the guy and started hitting him.

Charlie ran to Anna as Ben ran around the other side pulling the other guy out of the car and giving him a beating of his own.

In the distance, they heard a truck approaching and sirens as well.

Eric and Max jumped out of the truck with guns drawn and had to stop Ben and Wyatt from killing the two men.

* * * *

Stacy screamed then cried as she saw all the blood and Anna looking like she was dead on the ground.

Wyatt and Ben immediately went to Anna's side.

"Is she alive?" Wyatt demanded.

"I got a real weak pulse. Shit! Did you see how fucking hard he slammed her to the door. God, I think it's bad," Charlie stated.

"The ambulance is on its way," Eric added from a few feet away. Just then, three other patrol cars and the paramedics made their way across the field.

The paramedics were immediately by her side evaluating her injuries.

They listened as the paramedics spoke into their radios.

"We need a medevac ASAP. Patient in critical condition, large laceration plus swelling, unconsciousness, and dangerously low blood pressure. Surgeons on standby, ETA twenty minutes," the paramedic stated as they prepared to take Anna by helicopter.

"What's going on? What do they mean 'medevac'?" Stacy asked.

"What hospital are you taking her to?" Charlie asked.

"Memorial Hermann, sir," the paramedic responded, and Charlie felt his stomach clench. It was a great hospital known for treating everything from amputations, head and spinal injuries, to Lupus. But it was also an hour away.

A few minutes later, they could hear the helicopter approaching and beginning to land.

Ben, Wyatt, and Charlie kissed Anna before they rolled the gurney to the helicopter.

They weren't going to let anyone get on the helicopter.

Wyatt pulled out his badge.

"I'm the sheriff, and this is my woman. Please let me go with her so she's not alone?"

The pilot nodded, and Wyatt got on with Anna and the medic on board.

He locked gazes with his brothers and fought to keep the tears from flowing.

* * * *

"Let's get moving. It will take an hour to get to the hospital by car," Max stated.

"With a state police escort, it will take half the time," Eric countered as he hit the speed dial on his cell phone.

"Let's get back to the house, lock things up, and get to Anna as fast as we can," Charlie replied, and they all headed toward the vehicles.

Chapter 17

Wyatt sat in the emergency room waiting area for over an hour before his brothers and cousins arrived.

"How is she? What are they saying?" Charlie asked as he embraced his brother. Then Ben, Eric, Max, and Stacy followed suit.

He shook each of the deputies' hands one at a time then answered.

"I don't know anything yet. They rushed her inside and told me to wait here and that the doctor would be out to see me as soon as he could."

"Was she still unconscious?" Charlie asked.

Wyatt shook his head.

"Shit!" he exclaimed as he ran his hand through his hair.

"What, Charlie? Why did you ask that?" Stacy asked, placing her hand on his arm.

He looked at her, the sadness and concern apparent in his eyes.

"In a brain injury, the longer she remains unconscious, the worse her prognosis could be."

"That fucking asshole banged her head against the door frame so hard," Ben whispered, then swallowed hard and turned away from everyone. Wyatt saw the tears in his brother's eyes. He was about to lose it himself with worry over Anna.

"Let's not jump to conclusions. All we can do is wait until the doctor comes out and tells us more," Wyatt stated, and everyone agreed.

* * * *

It was a good two hours later when the waiting room filled with more visitors. Mary and Jack came by with food and drinks for everyone from Francine's. The workers from the ranch and a few other store owners and friends from town came in as well. When Doctor Jones arrived, he went right up to the front desk, smooth-talked the nurse, and was able to go into the restricted area where they weren't allowed to enter.

"Dr. Jones will get an update," Eric whispered to Stacy as he held her in his arms.

Everyone turned toward the door as Dr. Jones and another doctor dressed in scrubs came out. He looked a bit taken aback at the crowd.

Dr. Jones whispered something to him and pointed toward Wyatt, Ben, and Charlie.

"I'm Dr. Martin, brain injury specialist." He reached out and shook the men's hands one at a time.

"First, let me tell you that we are taking very good care of Anna. She is getting the best treatment, and we are thorough in our evaluations. The medevac paramedics explained how her injury occurred, which is important for me to know in order to evaluate her treatment and make certain she recovers."

"Did she gain consciousness?" Ben asked.

"No. Not yet, which is what I am most concerned over."

"Jesus! What else can you tell us?" Charlie asked.

"Is she going to be all right? Will she recover completely?" Stacy asked.

"I can't say with a hundred percent certainty that she won't have lasting side effects. She's very petite and to sustain such a blow as she did there are many concerns."

"Those being?" Wyatt asked.

"My first concern is that she is still unconscious. The longer she remains that way the more severe her injuries can be."

"My God! What about tests like CAT scans or MRIs," Stacy asked.

"We are in the process of doing those. So far, it doesn't appear that there are any contusions to the brain. Basically, brain contusions are bruises of the brain tissue that occur as a result of brain trauma. In some cases, brain contusions lead to hemorrhages that are absorbed into the brain tissue."

"Has the swelling gone down?" Dr. Jones asked.

"The swelling has remained the same since she arrived in the ER. As you know, Dr. Jones, brain contusions are localized, a characteristic that distinguishes them from concussions, which are more spread out. Once we do the CAT scans and MRIs, we should be able to rule this out."

"So we wait for the results of the tests?"

The doctor nodded.

"Can we see her?" Wyatt asked.

The doctor hesitated then looked at Dr. Jones.

"I suppose for a quick minute. No more than that. We should have the results from the tests soon, and then we'll determine what we need to do to help her recover."

The men shook his hand, then followed him to the ICU.

* * * *

The nurse told them one at a time, so Wyatt entered first, although Charlie and Ben could see her through the windows. She was covered in wires, her face battered and bruised. Wyatt's heart pounded in his chest. The thugs had beaten her before him, and the others knew she was in trouble.

They had failed to protect her when she needed them most. He swallowed hard, finding it difficult to not become emotional.

She looked so pale and fragile with all the wires hooked up to her. The beeping sounds filled the room. It was surreal and frightening. One look at the gash by her head and the swelling that the doctor was concerned about had Wyatt shedding tears.

He knew he had little time, so he wiped his eyes and leaned down to kiss her cheek below the bruise.

"I love you, baby. Please wake up and come back to us. I can't live without you," he whispered as the tears rolled down his cheeks and he walked out of the room.

* * * *

One look at his brother and Charlie felt like vomiting. He'd never seen Wyatt cry before.

He touched Wyatt's shoulder as he passed him, but Wyatt's head was down as he exited the ICU.

Taking a deep breath, Charlie walked into the room and stopped short at the sight.

"Oh, Jesus, Anna!" he whispered, covering his mouth as he absorbed the sight of tubes, bruises, and monitors beeping. The sound of her heart beating should have brought him some peace, but instead, it scared him. Her face had cuts and bruises on it, and the gash by her head had been stitched up and bandaged. He prayed that there wasn't any internal bleeding or brain injury. He clenched his fists as the tears rolled down his cheeks. He should have killed the fuckers. They had enough time to rough her up again, and he hadn't been there to protect her. He swallowed hard.

He slowly moved closer and touched her delicate hand then a finger that didn't have some sort of monitoring device on it.

He leaned down and kissed her lips gently, away from the cut there.

"I love you, baby. Please pull through. We need you."

Slowly, he stood up and exited the room, closing his eyes and inhaling as he made eye contact with Ben. Ben looked downright pissed off.

* * * *

Ben headed into the room and stopped short the second reality hit him in the face. His woman was lying there in pain and possibly with permanent injuries because of two New York fucking mobsters. He hoped that the whipping he put on the one asshole had the guy dying. He wouldn't give the piece of shit a second thought. His focus was on Anna and getting her to wake up.

He swallowed hard at the sight of her injuries but remained focused before he cried like a fucking sissy. He leaned down low and kissed her neck, the only uninjured part of her skin showing.

"Anna, you better wake your ass up real fast now, or I'm going to punish you and turn that pretty little ass of yours red as a stop sign. Damn it, I love you, I need you, and I ain't gonna stand for this nonsense. You are a strong woman, so get your shit together and wake up." He clenched his teeth and tried real hard not to let the tears loose.

The heart rate monitor increased, making a louder sound as the rate picked up pace.

Ben stood up straight as the nurse came in quickly, checking on Anna then the monitor.

"What did you do?" she asked abruptly.

He was suddenly feeling guilty for possibly making Anna's condition worse.

"Shit!" he exclaimed as he ran his hand through his hair. The nurse touched his forearm.

"No, sir, it's not a bad thing. Whatever you did or said seemed to get through to her somehow. Sit here and keep talking to her and doing whatever it was you did. I'm going to call the doctor."

"You better get my brothers. They helped, too," he stated.

Ben watched the nurse leave, and he was suddenly filled with confidence. He leaned down and whispered all the things he would do to Anna when he got her back home to the Triple C Ranch.

* * * *

Charlie and Wyatt were waiting outside the door of the ICU for Ben. They heard a lot of activity, and then the door opened and the nurse in charge of Anna told them to come back in.

Wyatt looked at Charlie and knew his brother was scared.

As they approached the room, there was Ben, leaning close to Anna, whispering to her.

"Your brother was talking to her and said something that had her heart rate increasing and showing signs that she may awaken. The sooner she does, the better off she will be."

Quickly, Wyatt and Charlie entered the room and stood beside their brother. There wasn't much room for them, but they made do as Ben explained what he did.

"Son of a bitch! Our woman is lying here with a possible fucking brain injury and you threaten to tan her backside!" Wyatt exclaimed in disbelief.

Ben smiled a shit-eating grin, then continued to whisper to Anna and caress her hand.

Wyatt took her other hand, and Charlie caressed her skin as they talked to her and added comments to Ben's outrageous sexual adventures he explained to participate in with Anna.

"If that nurse or doctor hears what we're saying, they're going to kick us outta here," Wyatt said then laughed.

"I don't care if they hear or not. I love her," Ben replied.

Wyatt and Charlie smiled.

"I love her, too," they both replied in unison then laughed.

Ben gently caressed her cheek and whispered. "That's right, Anna. You got three grown, macho men crying over you. That isn't an easy thing to accomplish, I'll have you know. And just for that, I'm going to add an additional spanking. You should realize now that we would do anything for your love and to keep you with us on the

Triple C." He paused a moment then looked at his brothers. "Anything for the love of Anna."

"Anything," Charlie added.

"Anything," Wyatt whispered.

When they looked down toward Anna, her eyes began to flutter open.

"She's awake!" Ben called out as the tears ran down his cheeks. There was no stopping them, and he didn't care. He knew at that moment that his Anna was going to be just fine.

Chapter 18

The days had passed with tests, tests, and more tests until, finally, the doctor was certain that Anna did not sustain any permanent damage. She did have a severe concussion, had vomited too many times to count, which lead to more medication and dehydration treatments.

She suffered from headaches, dizziness, and blurred vision, which the doctor said was normal and could last months following such an injury. He did, however, say that since there was no sign of amnesia that she should recover a hundred percent.

It had been a long, tiresome three weeks, but finally, she was going to be released from the hospital to go home and remain under the care of Dr. Jones as well as Dr. Charlie Cantrell.

Her men had remained by her side day and night in shifts, traveling the hour to take the others' places and still work and care for the ranch. In between, she had visits from Stacy, Eric, and Max as well as Jack and Mary. She had a family now that loved her and she loved them.

Jake and Vinny were prosecuted for their crimes of attempted murder, aggravated assault, and the murder of Hank Parker. Things had a way of working themselves out. After the beatings that Ben and Wyatt had put on Vinny and Jake, both men suffered broken jaws, broken ribs, and cuts and bruises to their bodies. By the time they got out of the hospital and were incarcerated, they were both murdered during a gang fight in the prison courtyard. The detectives from New York said the investigation into their deaths was still pending. At least now she could sleep at night knowing they could never hurt her or her family again.

* * * *

Anna lay on the bed after taking a hot shower and dressing in Wyatt's black sheriff's department T-shirt.

She loved the feel of being home, on the fluffy comforter in her men's home. They even placed vases of fresh wildflowers on the bedside tables and opened the windows to let the warm summer air into the room.

Just as she leaned back and closed her eyes, she heard the footsteps coming up the stairs.

"Anna!"

"Up here!" she called back, keeping her eyes closed and loving the sound of Ben calling her in their home and the comfort it gave her.

He entered the room, kicked off his boots, and slowly crept onto the bed. Then she heard more footsteps as both Wyatt and Charlie came in, with Wyatt still in his sheriff's uniform. He just left for work about thirty minutes ago, what the heck was going on?

Anna laughed as Ben slowly spread her legs and plopped his head down in between them.

"Hey!" she exclaimed as she grabbed his head to stop him although she didn't want to. She had been waiting for them to make love to her, but they were so afraid of hurting her. The cut on her head would look bad for months, so they should just get over it.

A look toward the other two and she was pleasantly shocked as they began stripping their clothes off at record speed.

"We spoke with Dr. Jones today and got the okay," Ben stated, raising one eyebrow and smiling so wide his dimples winked at her. Then his statement registered just as Ben licked her folds, plunged his tongue inside her channel then nibbled her clit.

Wyatt climbed onto the bed, his engorged cock bobbing against his stomach as he took her lips into his mouth and sucked them. He put the French in French kiss as he twirled his tongue and pushed deeper, making her hold his head and reciprocate.

She felt Charlie on her other side as he tapped her cheek and Wyatt released her to suck on her neck and then her breast. Charlie held his cock in his hand, pumping it as he rubbed her other breast.

"Fuck, baby, you taste so good. I missed these meals," Ben stated as he sat up and began pulling off his clothes.

The men moved her to their liking, with Ben stretched out underneath her, pulling her down to straddle his cock. She took him inside, threw her head back, and moaned at the delightful sensation.

"God, I missed you," she whispered as he pulled her nipples, causing her to come forward and press against his chest.

"I missed you, too, baby. You feel so tight and hot. I love you," Ben said then pulled her down to him for a kiss.

She felt Wyatt behind her rubbing his fingers over her pussy then through the crevice to the puckered hole. One push inside and he switched from finger to cock, thrusting into her to the hilt.

Anna screamed and lifted her chest as Ben and Wyatt began to push in and out of her.

She opened her eyes, seeking out Charlie, grabbed his cock, caressed it then sucked him in deep, feeling just as frisky as her men.

"Fuck, I love this ass, and I love you, baby!" Wyatt yelled as he pounded in and out of her.

She moaned against Charlie's cock, sucking and pulling as her body heated up, prepared to explode at any second.

Charlie grabbed her hair and pressed forward, speeding up his pace. He was hard as a steel rod, but she kept up with him, her body rocking every which way.

"I love this fucking mouth, Anna," he screamed his release and exploded inside of her.

As he panted, holding Anna's head, she licked him clean.

"I love you, baby," he whispered as she released him then he kissed her mouth.

Wyatt picked up pace, countering to Ben's thrust, and she felt herself tighten and coil up inside.

Smack!

Anna screamed, shocked at the slap to her ass, which instantly sent her over the edge screaming her release. Then came Wyatt, and last was Ben panting out of breath.

As they slowly pulled from her body and she remained wrapped in Ben's arms, he whispered loud enough for his brothers to hear.

"I win this time, sweetheart," he teased then caressed the globes of her ass.

Anna leaned up on one elbow, then slowly glided her hand down his torso to his cock and balls. She gave them a squeeze as she licked his nipple and nibbled, pulling a little harder than he expected.

"Hey!"

"It's on," she purred then slithered down his body, taking Ben into her mouth. Charlie and Wyatt chuckled.

"Anna...remember those punishments we mentioned in the hospital..." Ben teased. His focus completely on Anna. She widened her eyes then smiled around Ben's cock as she continued to suck and raised her ass in the air toward the others.

"Hot damn, woman!" Charlie yelled.

"That looks like a challenge to me," Wyatt exclaimed then took position behind Anna, caressed each globe as he kissed each cheek, prepared to take her from behind.

Anna moaned.

"I think she likes that," Charlie stated.

"Well, I aim to please, especially when it comes to our Anna," Wyatt whispered then pushed forward, thrusting into her.

* * * *

Anna smirked as she relished in the sensation of being loved by her men. Whether they knew it or not, they were wrapped around her heart. Anna was grateful for a second chance at life and that they were together, that she finally had a home and a place where she was loved.

She also knew, since their first night together, that she would do anything for the love of Charlie, Ben, and Wyatt Cantrell. They were her cowboys, and she would love them, cherish them, and tease them every step of the way and especially in the bedroom.

THE END

WWW.DIXIELYNNDWYER.COM

ABOUT THE AUTHOR

People seem to be more interested in my name than where I get my ideas for my stories from. So I might as well share the story behind my name with all my readers.

My Momma was born and raised in New Orleans. At the age of twenty she met and fell in love with an Irishman named Patrick Riley Dwyer. Needless to say, the family was a bit taken aback by this as they hoped she would marry a family friend. It was a modern day arranged marriage kind of thing and my Momma downright refused.

Being that my Momma's families were descendents of the original English speaking southerners, they wanted the family blood line to stay pure. They were wealthy and my father's family was poor.

Despite attempts by my grandpapa to make Patrick leave and destroy the love between them, my parents married. They recently celebrated their Sixtieth wedding anniversary.

I am one of six children born to Patrick and Lynn Dwyer. I am a combination of both Irish and a true southern belle. With a name like Dixie Lynn Dwyer it's no wonder why people are curious about my name.

Just as my parents had a love story of their own I grew up intrigued by the lifestyles of others. My imagination as well as my need to stray from the straight and narrow made me into the woman I am today.

Also by Dixie Lynn Dwyer

Were She Belongs

Available at
BOOKSTRAND.COM

Siren Publishing, Inc.
www.SirenPublishing.com

LaVergne, TN USA
18 February 2011
217196LV00004B/218/P